SEALED AND DELIVERED

BY
JILL MONROE

First published in Great Britain 2010
Harlequin Mills & Boon Limited,
Eton House, 18-24 Paradise Road, Richmond, Surrey TW9 1SR

© Jill Floyd 2009

ISBN: 978 0 263 88149 3

14-1110

Harlequin Mills & Boon policy is to use papers that are natural, renewable
and recyclable products and made from wood grown in sustainable forests.
The logging and manufacturing processes conform to the legal environmental
regulations of the country of origin.

Printed and bound in Spain
by Litografia Rosés S.A., Barcelona

Jill Monroe makes her home in Oklahoma with her family. When not writing, she spends way too much time on the internet completing "research" or updating her blog. Even when writing, she's thinking of ways to avoid cooking.

Thanks again to Pink, my amazing daughters and all my family for their support.

To Gena Showalter—may everyone have a friend as good!

Thanks to Kassia Krozser who's been with me from the beginning—some day I promise to put in a serial comma, and you'll know that's for you.

For technical help, I often turned to Helen Kay Dimon and James Miyazawa—thanks so much to the pair of you.

Alison Kent, Betty Sanders, Donnell Epperson, Sheila Fields, Stephanie Feagan and Wendy Duren all allowed me to bounce an idea off of them, and I appreciate it so much.

Many thanks to both Kathryn Lye and Deidre Knight.

Prologue

NEW CITY. NEW LIFE. New bookstore.

Same old, same old, in the self-help section.

Hailey Sutherland ran her fingers along the familiar titles; most of these books she already owned.

Maybe the Problem IS Your Sex Life.

Owned it. And yeah, the problem probably *was* her sex life, in that she always picked complete jerks to have it with.

Make Love Happen to You.

Yeah, as if women hadn't been trying to make *that* reality for centuries. Besides, the book was mainly a bunch of self-esteem exercises. She and her self-esteem had come to an understanding some time ago. They loathed one another.

Becoming the Woman You Are Meant to Be.

"Come to mama," Hailey whispered as she pulled this new book from off the high shelf. She thumbed through the glossy pages. Personality quizzes, wish-list management sheets, projection tips… With a sigh, Hailey returned the book to the shelf. She'd done it all before.

Yet, here she was again in the bookstore looking for the answer. Her cell phone rang just as she was returning the book to the shelf.

"Hailey, you won't believe it. I've just booked a wedding shower in the Tea Room," gushed her sister, Rachel. She'd always been the enthusiastic one.

"I don't believe it," Hailey deadpanned.

"Well, believe it, and I'm going to need you to stop at the paint store on the way back home."

"So you finally decided on a color?"

"Papaya Whip."

"Sounds yummy."

"I think it's as close to the original color as we're going to get," she said with a heavy sigh. Her sister's search for *the exact same shade* that highlighted the Tea Room's ornate wooden scrollwork since the 1920s had been mercenary. Just like Hailey, Rachel had returned to The Sutherland a few months ago to take away control of their family bed & breakfast from the management company they'd hired after their parents' death five years ago.

Management company, what a joke. They'd mainly managed to run the place into obscurity and out of cash. But Hailey and Rachel were determined to change that. The B&B had kept generations of Sutherlands off the streets and employed, and it wasn't going down on their watch.

"With only two weeks, it'll have to do," her sister continued.

Hailey almost dropped the phone. "Did you say two weeks? As in, we're hosting a wedding shower in the Tea Room in two weeks?" Her stomach began to hurt.

"I had to take the booking," Rachel defended without sounding defensive. "You know how much we need the cash." Enthusiastic and practical…that was her baby sis.

With fewer and fewer reservations, her sister's now exhausted savings caught them up on the pile of unpaid bills the management company had left them with. Hailey's "rainy day" was to cover the soon-to-be established marketing plan that would return The Sutherland to San Diego's preeminent social spot.

At one point the Tea Room in The Sutherland had been *the place* for showers and parties in this area of California. It seemed a lot more doable three months ago. "Okay, but two weeks? We've never hosted anything like that before."

Rachel groaned into the phone. "Come on. You've been engaged three times."

"True, but all I had to do was show up for those parties."

"I'm sure something rubbed off. We can do it, Hailey. Look how easy everything has gone so far. We were both between jobs at the same time so we could come back and take advantage of that nice little loophole that let us drop the management company as if it's hot."

"You're still doing the song-lyric thing," Hailey teased. After gradation, Rachel had grabbed her guitar and drove herself to Nashville to try and make it as a songwriter. Song titles often made it into her everyday conversation.

Rachel ignored her and went on. "It's as if fate wants us to revitalize The Sutherland."

Fate and a lot of hard work.

"Okay, paint store it is," Hailey agreed and she closed her cell phone. She turned on her heel, nearly running into a large cardboard display. Overhead, a flashy red banner hung from the ceiling proclaiming, Don't Wait On Fate—Jump-Start Your Life Today!

Fate.

Strange, her sister had just mentioned the word and here she was almost being attacked by it. The display was talking her language. Jump-start life—sounded like self-help to her. Although what awaited her inside the cardboard display was not a book, but rather a deck of cards. Fate Delivery Cards. Somehow those cards managed to make their way onto the counter and into her bag with a colorful and very detail-oriented book on ceramic tile—the real reason for her trip to the store.

And since she was in the mood, she'd chalk her purchase up to fate, rather than poor impulse control.

1

NOT EVEN THE SOUND of footsteps echoed in the Naval Special Warfare Center as Lieutenant Commander Nathanial "Nate" Peterson led his trainees through the corridor. Each exercise had grown steadily more dangerous, and even though they'd gone over every aspect in the classroom, actuality always heightened the senses. Made the tension more acute.

"Where's the party?" a trainee called laughingly from the back. "I hear you always know."

Nate's shoulders straightened. Strange thing about tension…some soldiers rose to the challenge, some men snapped and some, well, some of them bellowed smart-ass remarks to their superior.

"You're never going to live that reputation down." Riley laughed quietly beside him. Their steps slowed as they approached the locker area where the men would change into their wetsuits.

Nate shot a disgusted look at the man he'd known since their BUD/S training class. True, Nate had earned a reputation as a man who liked to play hard but he worked just as hard. Harder, actually. And yes, he always knew where the party was. But there was something all SEALs understood, and that was to keep priorities in order.

Something that smartass hadn't yet realized. Some men knew and understood from the beginning when to turn *it* off and on. Others needed that knowledge worked into their thick heads. Like the Ensign behind him. As it had been for Nate a few years back.

Nate stopped, and turned to stare at the man who'd called the question, not needing to see the man to know who he was. Harper treaded toward a familiarity he hadn't yet earned. "Maybe a party isn't what you should be concerned about, Ensign Harper. Your swim time is slipping."

The younger man's back stiffened, and the other trainees hustled quickly into the locker room.

"So's your conditioning," Nate added. This next minute would be crucial. How Harper handled the criticism would prove to Nate if that man had what it took to earn his Trident. SEALs took evaluation and adapted and made themselves better.

The Ensign swallowed. "I've passed."

Eight years ago Nate *was* this guy, with his BUD/S, Hell Week and Jump School behind him. All that stood in the way between the Ensign and the Trident that turned a man into a SEAL was The Finishing School or the official name—SEAL Qualifications Training, here on Coronado. With the end prize in sight, that was something a man could get cocky about. But that cockiness *would* be a downfall…no question about it.

Although surely *that* had been long gone in Nate by the time he'd hit SQT. Some hardass instructor had ensured it. A man lost his swagger when he was wet, cold and covered in sand. Lost the arrogance, because his life, and that of his Team, depended on professionalism not ego.

Now it was his turn to make sure these men thought only of focus and discipline, and each other, not themselves.

Unfortunately.

"*Minimum* standards are forty-two pushups in two minutes. You content with the minimum?" Nate asked.

Something stony and strong-willed flared inside the other man's eyes. *Good.* "No sir," he answered, with nothing but determination in his voice.

No sir was right. Harper might just be the best man to come out of this class.

"Suit up," Nate ordered and turned, not waiting for a response. Their next drill was in an hour.

Once the candidates were out of earshot, Riley glanced at him. "How do you keep a straight face during that?"

Nate let his guard down a little and smiled. "By counting the hours until I'm out of here," Nate told him as they continued down the hall, just the two of them. "Besides, if I'm not on the Teams, I'm damn well going to make sure my replacement can do the job."

"Still doing the physical therapy?" Riley asked.

Nate shrugged. Three months ago, he'd been injured while rescuing a pirated freighter with rigged explosives. Now another man had his spot on his Team. While Nate was teaching. The muscles of his right leg cramped, and he breathed through his nose. *Control.*

But as soon as he was healthy, goodbye settling for being an instructor, goodbye Coronado Island, goodbye San Diego.

"If it's any consolation, I've heard good things about the training you're providing. I guarantee your fresh-off-deployment perspective will save a life."

He knew what Riley was trying to do, and appreciated the effort but men didn't join the SEALs for a pat on the back. Most of the stuff he and his fellow SEALs had done was so covert the files wouldn't be opened until he was long gone. Little would ever make the history books.

But Nate's friend did point out a reality. In another year, these men might be beside him down range. Most of these men he'd be happy to serve next to as SEALs… but they weren't there yet. He might not like instructing, but he'd make damn sure the new guys wouldn't hold a Team back. They'd be ready on day one. "So is there a party?" Riley asked hopefully.

"After this exercise, I'm on my way to pick up the beer," he said, with a wink.

"Hoo yah."

"WHOO HOO! NAKED!"

The echoes of laughter flowed from the newly-re-painted Tea Room into the modernized kitchen. Hailey glanced at her sister Rachel and smiled. "Those are the sounds of a good party."

"I have to hand it to you, Hailey. You did a great job with this wedding shower."

"As you've pointed out, I've had three. Glad something useful came out of those relationships." With a flourish, Hailey topped the last of the mousse with chocolate shavings. "Of course you can't really go wrong with chocolate and champagne."

"Or naked beefcake."

"I don't think The Sutherland is quite ready for that." Hailey lifted the tray and scooted backwards, pushing the door out into the Tea Room with her backside.

"The chocolate's here!" called Amy Bradford, the bride to be. Although they'd been friends since school, they'd lost track of each other. Reuniting with old pals was another positive she could attribute to returning home.

"Wait," said a redhead, who Hailey had learned was the maid of honor. "The girls and I chipped in and bought you something to wear on your wedding night." The other guests met this announcement with everything from giggles to a few oohhs. In a flourish, she presented to the bride a large paper-wrapped box tied with a bright yellow bow.

"Five bucks says that box is empty," Rachel whispered.

Hailey glanced at the dozen or so women. Despite their pastel sundresses, these ladies looked like they were up for a little mischief. Hailey shook her head. "Not taking that bet."

Careful not to rip the ribbon, the bride did indeed open an empty box to the laughter of the group. With the last present now revealed, Hailey and her sister moved forward to serve the desserts. The rest of the guests made room on the table for the treat their little B&B had always been known for in decades past.

Amy glanced up toward Hailey. "I can't tell you how excited I am that you have reopened The Sutherland. When I was seven and a flower girl, my aunt had her shower here."

"Amy's had her heart set on this place ever since," the maid of honor added. "I couldn't believe my luck when I found out you just happened to have a free weekend."

The two sisters looked at one another. Yeah, they had plenty of free weekends. But it was nice to keep up the illusion of exclusivity.

"It was fate," Amy said with the kind of beaming smile only a woman about to be married could get away with.

Had Hailey ever worn such an expression at any of *her* wedding showers? She doubted it.

"And the Tea Room looks just as beautiful as I remember," Amy continued.

"Tell your friends," Hailey encouraged, ever the businesswoman, and ready to tear her thoughts away from her failed engagements.

After serving the ladies, and refreshing their tea, Hailey and Rachel began to discreetly clear away the wrapping paper. "I can't tell you how relieved I am," Rachel said quietly. This was the first real test of their hosting skills. While The Sutherland had been in their family for generations, and they'd performed their fair share of serving, their mother had always been the hostess.

Just to make sure the place shined, the last coat of paint to the Tea Room had gone up sometime around two that morning. Now looking around the beautiful banquet hall, Hailey experienced a swell of pride to see her home restored to as close as the sisters could remember it. The cypress wainscoting she was never allowed to touch gleamed. Prisms of light reflected around the room from the newly washed crystals hanging from the chandelier. The cornice molding gleamed with its new coat of papaya whip.

She just hoped no one looked under the crisp linens because the tables were a disaster. The management team apparently held an aversion to coasters. After hearing the delight of their new guests, the memory of all their hard work faded away. Grandpa Sutherland would be proud.

"This dessert is to die for," one of the ladies exclaimed.

Hailey winked at her sister.

"What's next?" asked another guest.

The smile faded from her sister's face.

The bridal party had already played Groom Trivia, Wedding Night Surprise, opened the presents and consumed dozens of champagne soaked strawberries. Hailey had heard so many off-color wedding night jokes, she could probably start a stand-up routine. "What's next?" her sister mouthed.

After being awake for nearly twenty-four hours, Hailey had hoped it was a nap.

The bride had mentioned something about fate, and ding ding ding, that little word triggered a memory in her sleep deprived and work fogged brain of a bookstore purchase not so long ago. So far fate had worked on their side, maybe they should keep it rolling. "Our *last* game will be ready as soon as we've cleared," Hailey told them demurely, then turned to race up the stairs two at a time to her bedroom. If her grandma had seen her run through the hallway like that…

Four months ago, the funding for her junior assistant curator position at the Dallas Museum of Art ran out, leaving her jobless. Back in San Diego, she'd reclaimed the bookshelf-lined room that had been hers. The corner room with a small window to the ocean had been her refuge from the oh-so-embarrassing job of working in her family's B&B when she was growing up.

While her friends were hitting the sandy beaches,

she'd been learning the secrets to making spider web Grenache, or worse, taking care of the guests' laundry. She smiled at the memory of her teen angst. What she wouldn't give now to sit beside the large stove and talk to her mother as she made the delicious meals for their guests, or hear her grandma's lessons of how a real lady crossed her legs at the ankle.

A time when she didn't have to worry about bills. Hailey wouldn't lose the battle for The Sutherland before she'd really had a chance to implement her ideas. Growing up in a work of art, like The Sutherland, with so much history, it was no wonder she'd been drawn to preserving and showcasing the past. Now she was saving something infinitely more personal…her family's legacy. Though she had work to do on the first step— save this wedding shower. She scanned the various self-help titles that now filled her bookshelf, looking for the bright red packaging. There they were—the Fate Delivery cards.

She peeled off the plastic wrapping as she raced down the hallway, stuffing the cellophane wrapper into her apron. Hailey plastered on a serene expression reminiscent of their mother as she returned to the Tea Room where Rachel finished the last of the clean-up. Their guests were talking quietly, looking over the various gifts the bride had received.

Needing to set some kind of mood here, Hailey flipped the switch cutting off the light provided by the chandeliers. The natural sunlight filled the room with its warm tones.

"Okay, ladies, the time is now," she said, her voice low and laced with dramatic flourish. An instant hush fell over the room. Hey, they were into it. Maybe Hailey had finally found the silver lining of taking that acting class in college, which sadly had led her to Fiancé Failure Number One.

"Amy is about to embark on a new journey that fate has ordained. Now it's our turn to see what's destined for the rest of us." Hailey fanned the cards in her hand. "Pick your fate, but don't look at it."

Each guest in the circle took a card, holding it to her chest, giggling to one another about taking peeks. Hailey held out the deck to Amy.

"Maybe I shouldn't take a card," the soon-to-be-bride said.

"Oh, take a card, Amy," said the maid of honor with a quick nudge. "It's just a game."

With a good-humored smile, Amy slid a card from the deck and placed it face down on her lap.

Hailey returned the unused cards back in the cardboard box they came in and set them aside. "Now ladies, the bride will choose who goes first," she instructed, making the rules up as she went. "You will show your card to the rest of the group, then look at it yourself. Some of the fates are silly and fun, but others are true life-changing destinies."

She hoped.

Maybe.

Hailey backed away to the wall where her sister watched. "Fate had ordained?" Rachel whispered to her. "I've forgetten how dramatic you can be."

"If it works, it works. Did you catch my emphasis on the word *last,* when I talked about this game?"

"Here's hoping they did," Rachel said, hiding a yawn with her hand.

"Tori, you go first," Amy said, clearly fired up to get this game going.

Tori turned her card to show to the rest of the group. A few groans followed.

"Oh, you have an easy one," one of the ladies called out.

Tori twirled the card around and read aloud. "Kick off your shoes and run into the wind." Then she glanced at her friends, raising a brow. "Speak for yourself on that being easy. Once I get these heels off, they're not going back on."

"No, you can't get out of it," Amy insisted, now fully involved in the game. "The beach is right outside this window."

Floor to ceiling windows dominated one side of the Tea Room. Shrouded in beautiful lace, the curtains allowed natural sunlight to filter into the room. But sweep them aside, and the Italian tiled terrace beckoned, as did the beach. The perfect place to kick off shoes and run.

"I'll handle this," Hailey said as she pushed off the wall and walked to the curtains that hid the glass door to the terrace. After draping the heavy material in the ornate holdbacks, she unlocked the doors so the women could step outside.

"Oh, this is beautiful," several of the guests murmured as they stepped out onto the terrace, their heels clacking on the original tile some Sutherland relative had installed. She and Rachel hadn't done much to this area but clean up the landscaping, although her sister had big plans to add tables and chairs, and serve brunch accompanied by an ocean breeze. There were other ways for the B&B to earn money besides guests in the rooms.

"Tori, just because it's pretty out here doesn't mean

we've forgotten why we've come. You've got some running to do."

With a sigh, Tori reached down and slid the straps off her heels, and carefully tucked her shoes to the side. "Here I go!" she called out.

Hailey had to join in the laughter as Tori took off down the beach in her sundress, the wind blowing in her hair. She turned to run backwards, raising her hands in the air like a winning marathon winner.

"Oh, no. Tori, look out."

But Tori was too far away to hear Amy's warning call, and Tori jogged right into the very solid chest of a man enjoying the beach with his dog. Now off balance, Tori began to slide to the sand until the man dropped his Frisbee and caught her. He steadied her against his body.

Amy's warnings turned to laughter as Tori glanced up to her savior's face. Then smiled. Slowly. The man didn't let go.

"Get his name," one of the guests called.

"And his number," Amy added.

"I tell you, she meets men in the weirdest ways," said the maid of honor. "Amy, choose who should go next."

Amy glanced over at Tori, who was now tilting her head and brushing sand off the man's arm. "Should we wait for her?"

"No, that's going to take awhile. Look at him, he's a goner."

With a nod, Amy agreed. "Then you should go."

Just as the maid of honor was about to reveal her card, her cell phone rang. Looking down at the display she frowned. "Amy, I'm sorry, I have to take this." The maid of honor thrust the card toward Hailey and quickly made her way back inside the Tea Room.

"Oh, but—" Hailey stammered.

"Show it, Hailey," Amy said.

Hailey glanced across the veranda to the Tea Room. It didn't appear as if the maid of honor was coming back any time soon. Well, Hailey had bought these cards for a reason. Maybe now it was time to do something for herself. With a sigh, she turned the card toward her guests.

To a lot of laughter.

"Oh, that's hilarious."

"That could be really good or really bad."

With some alarm, Hailey quickly turned the card over and read, "Kiss the first man you see."

No. NO. And hell no. Getting away from men was the second reason she'd come home. Hailey wasn't about to actually throw herself at one. And, as far as she was concerned, certainly nothing good ever came from kissing.

Some of the women were already moving toward the end of the terrace to search the sandy beach for available men, their skirts twirling in the breeze. "I see a few contenders way down the beach," one said, smiling.

"Just think, five minutes earlier and it would be *you* in the arms of that guy instead of Tori," said another.

Tori was welcome to him. To all men.

A strange whooshing sounded over their heads. Hailey's skirt practically lifted to her chin thanks to a strong, very out-of-place gust of air. Okay, not completely out of place. Shielding her eyes with one hand, and trying to hold strands of her carefully constructed chignon in place, Hailey looked up to spot the now familiar helicopter hovering over the ocean.

The Navy SEALs were back.

Hailey suppressed a groan. The SEALs had been conducting their training nearby on a semi-regular basis ever since she'd returned to Coronado. But Saturday afternoons had always been blissfully free of the noise and the wind. Why now during their first formal event?

The door of the helicopter's cabin slid open sharply and some kind of rope was thrown out, the end suspended just a few feet above the water.

"What's going on?" asked a guest.

"Would anyone like more tea?" Hailey tried, but no one was paying her any attention. Everyone's focus was on the chopper.

At the cabin's entrance, a man emerged, clad in a skintight black wetsuit. Hell, she might as well look, too. She squinted, but Hailey was too far away to make out features. Besides, she was paying too much attention to the fact that he was solid, lean muscle. She swallowed as he caught and pulled the rope toward him, wrapping it around his wrists and hands while securing it with his long legs. Hailey gasped as he flung himself over the side of the helicopter, strength evident in his every move. Her mouth went dry as he slid down the rope, heading for the rough, churning water. When he reached the end of the rope, he dove into the ocean, leaving little splash.

"Did you see that?" one of the women asked, her voice hushed.

How could she not?

After a moment he resurfaced, and the breath she'd been holding finally released.

"I'd think that would qualify as the first man you see,

Hailey," Rachel said, not able to suppress the laughter from her voice.

"Hope you have a nice bikini to wear to swim out there to meet him," the bride said, joining in the fun. "But look."

With reluctance, Hailey took her gaze off the man easily treading in the ocean to find even more men scrambling out of the helicopter.

Great. This was just great. The last thing she wanted to do was kiss a man, and fate had sent them literally falling out of the sky.

2
_____

"WHICH ONE ARE YOU GOING to choose?" Rachel asked, her voice filled with laughter. Gleeful, encouraging-of-others to torment her sister kind of laughter. Now Hailey didn't feel so bad about the "haircut" she'd given Rachel at the age of four.

"Five, six, seven," Amy counted as each man pro-pelled himself onto the rope. "And they keep coming. So would the first one technically be the first one out of the helicopter?"

"I have a self-help book that would be perfect to cure you of that sarcasm. It means you're hiding a lot of pain," Hailey whispered to her sister.

"Nah," Rachel said with a growing smile.

"No, I think it would be the first one she'd reach," said another guest.

"Well, that could depend on which direction she swam, giving her a choice."

These ladies were applying the same kind of argu-ments and logic one would use when discussing String Theory or macroeconomics. It was just a guy.

"So which one?" Amy asked.

Curious eyes now gazed her way.

None of them.

Thankfully, the whooshing sounds from the helicopter drew their guests' attention away from her.

"Oh, they're leaving," one of the ladies said, clearly disappointed.

"Just the helicopter. The guys are still in the water. Look."

Sure enough eight men waded in the water. Sometimes they would point, or go under the waves for a moment, but basically stayed in the same general location, performing what looked like drills.

"Now that can't feel good. The water is cold this time of year. Why would they be out there?" asked one of the women, frowning.

The bride leaned forward. "One word—training. Those are Navy SEALs."

"SEALs?"

The sisters nodded in confirmation. They'd witnessed this little scenario play out with several of their female tourists. First the confusion, then the excitement followed by the gawking.

"Why didn't you say so before?" Two of the women rushed to the railing to get a closer look, their heels clacking against the tile. *Yeah, it was pretty much downhill from here.*

"I didn't realize you could see them from the B&B."

"All up and down this area. They train right on Coronado," Hailey told them.

One woman, who Hailey thought might be the guest book attendant, pulled out her camera phone and snapped a picture.

"What's going on?" Tori asked. She'd left her new

friend, slipping a note inside her purse as she rejoined the group.

Amy looped her arm through Tori's and led her to where she could see the beach. She pointed out toward the water. "Hailey's fate is to kiss one of them."

"Lucky her," Tori said, turning appreciative eyes out to the ocean.

Amy propped her hand on her hip. "Didn't you just have a bit of luck yourself? Was that a phone number I saw you squirreling away?"

A slight flush touched Tori's cheeks. "I have a date Friday night."

"Tori, you're the only person I know who could snag a date at a wedding shower."

This *had* to be good for business. Following clean up, and a nap, Hailey would be buying more sets of cards. After she ducked out on fulfilling the dictates of the card thrusted upon her, that is.

Amy put an arm around Hailey's shoulder. "I see you backing away. Don't think we forgot about you, kiddo. You still have a Fate waiting for you."

When had the bride become so menacing? Maybe Hailey wouldn't be buying those additional decks after all.

"Come on, ladies, you know I'm not swimming out there," she told them, with a touch of fun firmness that said she understood she was in on the joke.

"Maybe you won't have to," Tori said, pointing at the ocean. Two of the men had broken away from the group and were now swimming straight for The Sutherland. Straight toward her.

Hailey's eyes widened as she realized one of them wasn't swimming, and appeared to be unconscious. She sucked in a breath, then watched in amazement as the swimmer rolled the other onto his back, then secured the inert man to his side. With strong sure strokes, he headed for shore. Swimming from that distance would have been exhausting, but pulling the weight of another full-grown man must have been almost impossible. She scanned the beach for some kind of boat. Maybe she could meet them half way.

Kicking off her heels, she lifted her skirt and flew down the tiled stairs of the terrace to the sand below.

"Looks like she found her kissing candidate." Whistles and catcalls from the shower guests followed Hailey onto the beach.

"Call 9-1-1," she hollered and she raced toward the man, kicking up sand behind her.

"What?" The ladies' teasing turned into murmurs of concern.

The swimmer was now standing waist deep in the water. She'd never seen anything like him. Clad shoulder to foot in a dark, skintight wetsuit, he emerged from the ocean. The powerful muscles of his thighs flowed with strength. His suit outlined every solid ripple of the lean lines of his shoulders and arms. He reminded her of Colossus, the powerful X-Man who transformed into solid, dark steel. Her second fiancé sold a ton of those comic books in his store, and witnessing someone with such a show of strength in aid of another, she understood Colossus' appeal.

The SEAL's burden still hadn't moved, and her breath shallowed in panic. The cool water of the Pacific splashed at her ankles as she raced to meet them.

"Stay back," he warned.

"Let me help," she offered, seeing the fatigue lining his face. "I'm stronger than I look."

At five feet two inches, she must look pretty scrawny to this big man. With a reluctant nod from him, she looped the injured man's arm around her shoulder, taking only a little of the weight. Colossus still managed the bulk of the load. "My friends are calling for help. 9-1-1," she added.

"I've already radioed for the helicopter."

"From in the water?" she asked, feeling almost instantly silly. Seeing the men up close in their wetsuits or rash guards or whatever they called that tight-fitting dive garb, there was no question they were military. Of course they had some kind of waterproof device. "I know CPR."

Colossus shook his head as they eased the man to the sand and positioned him on his back. "He's breathing. He hit his head and blacked out. I made sure he didn't take in any water."

"Oh," she said, sitting back on her heels, her breath coming out in little pants. Okay, well. Colossus seemed to have everything in hand. What was the protocol in a situation like this? Offer him some mousse as they waited for rescue? It didn't matter. He wasn't paying her any attention, instead checking on his fallen comrade, counting out his pulse against his watch and lifting the man's eyelids.

Water ran crazy paths down his forehead and cheeks, but he never brushed it away, utterly focused on the task at hand.

"Is there anything I can do?" she asked, wanting to help.

The man simply shook his head. He didn't seem to

mind the cold she knew he must be feeling. His breathing was heavy, but he hadn't handed over responsibility for the other soldier to her so he could take a break. His words had been confident, and his actions seemed to back him up. Unlike Fiancé Failure Number Three who never wasted an opportunity to offer an "expert" opinion, but was only adept at giving completely useless advice.

After a few minutes, the man beside her signaled to his crew still in the water. With a few waves of the hand, that Hailey was sure meant something, they continued on with whatever it was they were doing.

Now, after taking care of everything and everyone else, the SEAL lowered himself to the sand and stretched out his long legs. She tried to avert her eyes, she really did, but that dark wetsuit he wore like a second skin left nothing to the imagination. Actually, both her imagination and reality were enjoying a great show. He finally slicked the water from his face, then glanced her way. His eyes widened as if he was seeing her for the first time.

"Than—"

"Uhh," the man between them stirred, reaching toward his head. A trickle of blood mixed with the water from the ocean was beginning to trail down his temple.

"Don't touch."

"Try not to touch," she said, injecting calm into her voice.

They spoke at the same time. Only his words sounded more like an order.

The injured man blinked a few times against the sun, then his gaze settled on her. "What kind of salvation is this?" He slowly rubbed the saltwater from his eyes. "An angel, and my head hurts like a bi—"

"That's enough, Ensign Ortiz," Colossus said, authority lining every word.

The Ensign's gaze cut toward Colossus. "What happened?" he asked.

Yeah, she was curious about that, too.

"Head."

Okay, not helpful.

The man on the sand squeezed his eyes tight for a moment, took a deep breath and then with a force of will she'd never seen in another person, pushed himself up to a sitting position. "I'm ready."

It didn't fully sink in that the Ensign, who was unconscious only seconds before, had every intention of going back into the water. And that Colossus was going to let him. "But you can't," she said, scrambling to her feet. Colossus had already smoothly stood, his tall frame blocking the sun from her eyes.

"It's his job," Colossus told her.

With another show of will, the Ensign shoved to his feet. He barely remained upright, then gathered his balance steadily. "Ready," he repeated.

"Look this way," Colossus ordered. He examined the Ensign's eyes, his face relaxing a tick. "Knots on your head?" he asked.

The younger man felt along his scalp, shaking his head no.

Colossus angled his head toward the water. "Okay."

With a look of relief, the other man began to walk to the ocean.

"But he's bleeding," she protested.

"The saltwater will take care of his wound," Colossus stated, seemingly unconcerned.

She glanced back toward The Sutherland. "I have some anti-bacterial foam—"

Colossus's lips moved as if he was trying to suppress a smile. "He's trained to fight with worse."

She swallowed. Of course he was.

"I can't believe what he's doing," she said, watching the Ensign as he made a smooth dive into the waves, and swam toward the other men still treading water. "Maybe we should have waited until the paramedics arrived." Yet with every stroke he seemed to gain more strength.

"I've had combat medical training. I checked for signs of concussion. He's fine."

These men lived in a different world, far away from the corresponding bridal ribbons, chocolate shavings and the waterproof bandages she would have suggested next.

She turned away from the swimming soldier to face Colossus, and that's when her gaze collided with the steel gray of his. Her breath hitched. Sure she'd noticed the strength of his body outlined so perfectly in his wetsuit, his air of authority and control as he'd handled the situation with the injured soldier, but this man's eyes were something else. Something inviting and very, very sexy.

A cool breeze from off the ocean fanned her face, her bare arms. Although she tried to fight back a shiver, her nipples tightened. She hoped he'd think her bodily reaction was due to the weather and not the hot, suddenly carnal thoughts popping into her mind about him. Like running her fingers along his arm to feel the solidity of his muscles. To lick that drop of saltwater off his cheek. Or discover just how one gets a wetsuit off a man. Zipper? Scissors? Who knew?

No. No. And hell no. These thoughts were ending right here. She was not in the market for a fling. Or a boyfriend. Boyfriends tended to become fiancés in her world. This would make Fiancé Failure Number Four. And that she was finding someone attractive that she didn't normally go for meant nothing. In fact, her virtually nonexistent male filtering system had probably just widened the search parameters.

Then Hailey realized they'd both been standing facing one another far longer than necessary. A pause, a tension sprang up between them, and hung heavily in the air. His gray eyes narrowed, something deep in those depths flared. Her lips parted, and she acknowledged her urge to lean into him, get closer. His gaze flickered to her lips, then returned to her face.

And what that brief glance at her mouth did to her.

Go. Now was the time for him to leave. To turn around and head back to the ocean.

"I'm glad your friend is going to be okay." The words rushed out of her. Okay, so she wasn't actually ready to let him go. "That was pretty impressive what you did."

He shrugged, obviously uncomfortable with that tiny bit of praise.

"I liked the way you rushed to help." Not that she'd done much, but it was nice to hear.

She should be uttering a quick goodbye, and get back to her guests. But her gaze settled on his lips and a rush of warmth blasted through her.

You're supposed to kiss him.

That heat became a fire. What would his lips feel like? Did she dare? With the fate card in mind, Hailey gave herself permission to do what she really wanted to do all along. She followed that push to be closer, and found herself tilting slightly forward. His hands raised, and—

The sounds of giggles had her taking a quick step back. Hailey looked away from Colossus to see Amy, Tori and her sister carrying their shoes and casually making their way towards her and the Navy SEAL.

"Oh, Hailey. That is definitely 'first man you see' material," Tori teased.

In addition to the cards, this would be the last time they served champagne at any wedding showers.

"I've been keeping my eye on you, and you haven't fulfilled your fate yet," Amy said with faux sternness as she handed Hailey the card.

Hailey's gaze went to her sister who only shrugged and flashed her a smile. Why had she even bothered looking at Rachel for help? She was obviously getting a kick out of this.

Colossus was retreating, clearly confused by the conversation, happy not to get involved. "Thanks again for your assistance." He was all business now.

Hailey would just have to ignore that disappointment she felt at the loss of heat between them. Well, from his side. She was still very, very hot.

"Wait, you can't go." Amy's voice lifted higher on each syllable.

"Right," Tori said, lifting up her nearly empty champagne glass. "Hailey hasn't kissed you yet."

Colossus paused. He glanced her way. "You Hailey?" he asked, interest in his eyes.

Did she hear a hopeful tone in his voice? Dear God she hoped so. Hailey surveyed the ladies all eyeing her Navy SEAL. Amy lifted a brow, but her lips twisted in a smile.

They didn't think she was going to do it.

They weren't egging her on because they thought it was funny or were trying to encourage her. They were goading her because it would be even funnier when she *didn't* kiss him. Well, now. She was having none of that. Hailey hadn't read a dozen self-help books on visualizing the goal and actualizing, for nothing.

Goal = Navy SEAL's lips.

Now for the actualization part.

Hailey straightened her shoulders, determinedly took the two steps to reach the man's side and tugged on his shoulder until he fully faced her. Surprise widened his eyes, but that was the last thing she saw as she closed hers, stood on tiptoe and pulled him down to meet her mouth.

For a moment, he stood still, his lips warm, firm and unmoving beneath hers.

One. Two. Three seconds and she was done. Fate fulfilled.

But apparently fate wasn't done with her yet, because her Navy SEAL had just gripped her hips and crushed her to his chest. The water from his wetsuit seeped to her breasts, making her shiver, but she didn't care because his lips weren't unmoving anymore. They were opening and drawing a sweet response from hers. His tongue traced the seam of her mouth, and a deep longing flowed inside her.

He smelled of the sea and ocean air, and tasted of salt and delicious man. Hailey wanted nothing more than to keep kissing him as she sunk her fingers into his short hair, still wet from the swim. And just when she settled into the kiss, his hands began to roam.

Hailey's heart raced, her legs weakened and she

could think of nothing better than to keep doing what she was doing.

So that's why she pushed herself away.

That shove was an effort, but she took a step back, and their gaze collided. His face was tight, and desire burned in his eyes. Desire burning for her. She sucked in a breath, but walked away. If she kept looking at the clear hunger in his confused eyes, she'd be right back in his arms. Instead, she stopped at the three stunned ladies staring at her. Hailey gave them a breezy smile. "Done."

The sand sifted between her toes as she ambled slowly back to The Sutherland where the rest of the guests waited for her on the terrace. She swore she felt Colossus's gaze on her back as she walked away from him, but that was ridiculous.

"Wait, Hailey," she heard her sister call, but she kept on walking.

After grabbing her shoes, she ascended the steps. She was greeted by a mixture of uncertainty from the guests. And in herself. Her self-imposed male isolation hadn't done much by way of inoculating her from their sweet temptation.

The maid of honor was only then leaving the Tea Room with cell phone still in hand. "What'd I miss?"

Hailey's fist tightened around the Fate Delivery Card for a moment before she thrust it at the woman whose fate she'd just fulfilled. "Here's your card."

NAVY SEAL TRAINING HAD prepared Nathaniel Peterson for a lot of things. But after Hell Week, Phase Two, SQT and two deployments he shouldn't have been caught off guard when a beautiful woman kissed him.

And he'd stood there like an idiot when she'd walked off. The hottest, most unexpected kiss of his life, and he failed to follow up. He deserved to watch her walk away, but oh, how he would remember the sweet taste of her mouth and curves of her body pressed to him.

"I can't believe she did that?" said one of the women.

They traded incredulous glances between themselves then began to laugh.

Stop standing there like an idiot.

"Okay, well, bye," said the one woman with a bunch of mismatched ribbons in her hair. She caught the arm of the woman who'd called him "first man you see material" and the two of them followed along the same path his kisser had fled.

The last lady eyed him up and down. Then, with a nod to herself, she whispered, "Her name's Hailey. She works at The Sutherland." With a point at the large Victorian, she took off, following the others.

A slow smile spread across his face. How could he not appreciate it when the locals provided much needed intel? Or the way Hailey's skirt cupped her ass as she climbed the stairs away from the beach. With a shake of his head, he turned and sprang into action, hitting the waves and swimming back to his trainees.

They continued to tread water; this long and cold endurance exercise would prepare them for the water insertions they'd practice next. From the tight looks on his men's faces, they were fighting grins. And losing.

"That looked real dangerous."

"We were considering whether or not you needed backup."

Yeah, yeah yeah. He probably deserved the razzing. But should he end it? Instructing was still so new to him. Training was exhausting, stressful work, and handling a few cracks from another SEAL was a low price to pay for pushing them as hard as he did. Besides, he'd already played hardass once today.

"She need mouth-to-mouth?"

Low price to pay to a point. "Shut it, before I drown you."

The water grew choppy, which signaled the helicopter's return. The men were then forced to handle their communication by hand signals. It was just as well. Nate had a few hand signals in mind that weren't Navy regulated.

A rope ladder descended from their transport above, and Nate supervised as each man made his way safely out of the water. He gripped the rung, and hauled himself out of the water, his knee aching with the effort. He gritted his teeth and began to ascend the ladder. It was no secret to the men he trained he'd rather be out with his Team than in San Diego, but orders were orders, and he had enough discipline to admit that until he was fully healed, he'd be more of a hindrance than a help.

It still didn't make him wish for something different.

Nor did it stop him from glancing once more at the beach. Commander Nate Peterson knew three things: he was in for a longer stretch in San Diego than he'd planned, his need for the woman who'd kissed him hadn't lessened, and he *would* see her again. He'd make sure of it.

3

"YOU KNOW HE STOOD there even after you left. He watched you."

Hailey put down the dishtowel she'd been using to dry the pretty yellow-flowered china that Sutherlands had served delicious meals on for generations. Gripping the delicate plate between her fingers, she stared at her sister. "No, he didn't."

"I think he was waiting to see if you'd turn around or something," Rachel said as she wiped suds off a saucer.

"I'm going to swat you with this towel if you don't stop talking about it," she warned.

Rachel lifted her hands out of the soapy water in surrender. "Fine, don't believe me. I was just wondering if you wanted to rinse off or something since that was the most intense eye-screw—or do you prefer eye-loving since you're such a romantic—I've ever seen."

He'd watched her? Something warm and tingly shimmied down her back, and she blinked. What was that? Some kind of shiver of desire? Nope, not going to acknowledge it. Didn't happen. What shiver of desire? She should never have dissed fate.

"And then with the other girls laughing, it had to have been weird for him," her sister continued.

Nope, Hailey would ignore that twinge of guilt. He was a Navy SEAL, he could handle it. "I thought we were going to drop this subject," she said, pulling the newly rinsed saucer out of the water.

"I remember you suggesting it," Rachel said, grinning. "Who knows, he might sort of…show up. Or maybe you could stroll up and down the beach in case Mother Nature starts raining men again."

Hailey wouldn't even respond to that little bit of insanity.

But she'd lived with the woman beside her almost her whole life, and knew when her sister wasn't going to let something drop. She placed the newly dried china saucer in the cabinet above her head and faced Rachel. "Why are you pushing this? You know my track record. The last thing I need to be is within shouting distance of a man."

The playful look on her sister's face faded. "Maybe you need a little hair of the dog?"

"Like cures like? Use a man to get over a man?" Hailey shook her head. "No, thank you. I'm pretty sure that rationale is what got me engaged time number three."

Rachel reached over and squeezed Hailey's hand. "I hate seeing you this moody, Hailey. For a minute there, out on the beach, I saw the feisty, never-turn-down-a-dare Hailey. I miss her."

If she were being honest, Hailey would admit she missed her old self, too. But something wasn't right in her life. And hadn't been for a while. "Yeah, well, the old Hailey made great work of her life so far. Four years of college, a degree in Art Adminstration under my belt and where do I find myself? At a complete dead stop in my career and right back at the family business. Art's to be experienced. I should be out there working to bring the best collections to the people. Managing field trips and docents. Helping teachers present the arts in their classrooms."

"Maybe this is where you're meant to be," her sister said gently.

Hailey released a heavy sigh. "Even if I gave that some credence, which I don't, there's still the issue of my three failed engagements. And let's not forget, you were the first person to tell me how bad my taste is in men. So, no, we may miss old Hailey, but at the age of twenty-seven, I'm here to find myself and nothing is going to stop me no matter how great a kisser the man is."

Or how solid his chest.

Or strong his legs.

A little shiver fluttered through her stomach.

Rachel's lips twisted in a not-so-great effort at hiding another grin. "Did you say find yourself? Now you sound like crazy Aunt June. What happened to her?"

"I think she moved in with her sister. We called her cool Aunt June until then," she reminded her sister dryly.

Her sister propped a hand on her hip. "See? There's the old Hailey I missed."

"You missed sarcasm? Now shoo—the new Hailey has a lot of work to do. I want to finish these dishes, take a nap and tackle that new self-help book." And work on never thinking of that man and his dangerous kisses again.

"Okay, okay," Rachel said, sinking her hands into the soapy water.

They worked together in silence cleaning the last of the china. The very modern stainless steel commercial dishwasher took care of the rest of the party utensils and serving dishes, but the Sutherland china was always washed by hand.

"This kind of reminds me of mom," Hailey said.

"I was thinking the same thing. How many times did we talk about boys, and dates with our hands in this sink?"

"Lots." She smiled at the happy memory.

"So, he was a good kisser?" Rachel asked.

God save her, yes. "Stop," she said in exasperation, then swatted her sister with the towel anyway.

AFTER A CHECKING ON the Ensign and a quick debrief, Nate Peterson headed to the weight room. He worked to mask the usually slight limp to his leg, more pronounced after the arduous training swim and carrying the injured man's weight up onto the beach.

He willed the pain away.

He'd dealt with worse. Fought with worse. Soon, the wicked scar wrapping around his thigh would be the only evidence he'd ever been hurt. His leg injury might prevent him from running, but it couldn't stop him from strength training. Nothing would stop him from returning to SEAL condition and taking his rightful place in The Teams when he was called.

Nate may have been looking for an escape from his old man, but fate had looked out for him that day when he was in the Navy recruiter's office at the age of eighteen.

He wasn't half way through basic when Nate realized he'd found a home. The Navy provided rules and discipline, something he'd never experienced growing up. His father may have laughed, but Nate actually excelled when there was a level of expectation. He wasn't a benchmark kind of guy. If there was a challenge, Nate didn't just want to meet it, he wanted to surpass it.

With the SEALs being the most highly regarded and trained of all the Special Forces, Nate knew that Trident would one day be his. He wouldn't let something like an injury prevent him from doing what he was supposed to do.

He adjusted the weight for the reps to work his upper body. Almost every base he'd been assigned housed a weight room. Different locales, different climates, different languages…this room with its benches, mirrors and weights, was like coming home. Working out was as much a part of his normal routine as shaving or eating. Only the physical therapy exercises were new. The movements, which would return the tone and flexibility to his muscles, he kept to himself and performed away from the eyes of others.

Nate controlled his breathing as he lifted and lowered his arms. Muscle memory took over, and his mind began to wander. To telling eyes, and soft warm lips.

What the hell had that been on the beach? With familiar discipline, he'd kept his thoughts squarely on his tasks and his men. But now…now he allowed himself to remember. And think of her. Of the flowery scent of her mixed with the ocean breeze. Or the way she felt, soft and warm against him.

His thoughts quickly turned to another kind of workout all together. Finding the zipper on the back of her dress, and drawing it down. Sliding those slender, tantalizing straps off the smooth skin of her shoulders, and letting her clothes fall to the sand at their feet.

Why had she kissed him?

Who the hell cared?

Nate heard footsteps in the hallway. His few moments alone were almost over.

"It looked to me like she just pulled him over and kissed him."

Yeah, that's exactly how it happened.

"He didn't handle the attack so well," another trainee said as they entered the weight room.

The hell he hadn't.

"If she'd had a knife stuffed in her purse, he'd have been a goner."

She didn't have a purse. Just a thin, thin dress.

"Maybe it's new Navy protocol." The three men laughed. At his expense. He knew they were only blowing off steam. SQT was just as mentally demanding as Hell Week was physically demanding. But he'd lose their respect if he didn't call them on it. He realized now he'd made a mistake out there in the water.

Nate lowered the weight and it clanged. Three gazes whipped his way. Followed quickly by three alarmed faces. He met each man eye to eye. His message was clear.

"We didn't know you were here, Instructor."

"Obviously," he replied.

The three stood together, uneasy, but not letting one man take the heat. Whatever Nate had to dish out at them they'd take together. The Teams would do well with soldiers such as these. Like him, they'd had a tough afternoon in the water, and he was impressed by their drive to hit the weight room instead of their bunks.

One day he might be fighting alongside them. They'd learned what he needed them to know.

"It's always preferable to make nice with the locals,"

he told them honestly, then turned, letting these guys off the hook. Yeah, he was a SEAL, "instructor" didn't sit well with him.

Relieved releases of breath made him smile as he left the room. He liked the men he was teaching; he just didn't want to be teaching them. Nate knew he could better serve the Navy and do what he was meant to do *out* of the classroom. He rubbed at the muscles above his knee. Soon. He'd be out of here soon.

Besides, none of them had the sexiest woman in San Diego wrap her warm body against them and plant the kind of hot kisses a man usually thought about on long, arduous hikes out in the dessert. In fact, with their training, the men hadn't talked to the fairer sex in awhile. However, *he* wasn't in training. Nothing was holding him back.

Being laid up in Southern California hadn't been his idea, but like any tactical move, he planned to take advantage of it. He had the whole night ahead of him, and it was no secret SEALs worked best when the sun went down. And he knew just where to find her. Hailey of the Sutherland Hotel.

She was a woman worth missing a party for.

Hoo ya.

HAILEY COULDN'T NAP LONG. Luckily, her sister's work on their Web site had yielded a booking for the evening, and she needed to be up and ready to help them check in. Like most B&Bs, the Sutherland served a delicious breakfast, but it had become a tradition to serve a light spinach and basil quiche in the afternoon for guests weary from travel and reluctant to fend for food in a strange city. Just one of the small touches that built a hotel's reputation. Something the management company hadn't understood.

The guest doorbell rang. The poor thing still sounded rusty. Wiping her hands on the apron protecting her clothes from the food prep, she quickly made her way to the door. Opening it wide, she almost wanted to slam it shut as quickly as she could.

It was *him*. The SEAL she'd kissed on the beach a few hours ago. Well, of course it was him. She'd just stood there in the kitchen dissing fate and fate obviously didn't like it. Her payback was a gorgeous man at her doorstep while she looked horrible. Then the nerves kicked in and her heart turned all fluttery.

"I don't normally walk around wearing this," she managed, thinking it might work to draw his attention away from the blue and white checked bib-style apron monstrosity. The baby doll blue dyed bias tape was even fraying around the edges.

Yet if someone were keeping track of the absolute stupidest things to tell a man, that would probably make the Top Ten. Why hadn't he said anything?

His eyes crinkled in the corners, he almost smiled, and it was almost a little too much. Whatever. He hadn't been invited; anyway, it was his own fault he saw her with her hair lazily knotted on the top of her head with a pencil she'd found in the kitchen. It's just, why did he have to look so good?

Fate.

His hair, thick with water the last time she saw him, hadn't revealed its true color brown, with a few strands turned copper, probably from his days under the California sun. But those gray eyes of his, the color of steel were the same, and they burned into her right now.

Yeah…it was still there. That heat, that unyielding attraction that lay between them even before she kissed him, only grew now. Now that he was here in her home looking big and sexy and so, so kissable.

She didn't need to worry about the stupid apron, apparently he was thinking about that kiss they'd shared, too. The intensity of his eyes as they met hers told her what was on his mind. Her skin heated, and she felt a flush in her cheeks. His gaze dropped to her lips and she found herself holding her breath.

Her sister charged through the door that led to the laundry, singing a Prince song. Rachel fumbled awkwardly to a stop when she saw them both. "Oh, my God, you're the…you know, the SEAL."

"I am," he said with a nod. Hailey wished she could read his expression. Right now it was agonizingly neutral.

Her sister had never been subtle. Today she was perfecting her art of embarrassingly stating the obvious.

"But you can call me Nate rather than the SEAL."

Rachel laughed. "Kind of sounds like you should be balancing something on the end of your nose."

Hailey felt sick to her stomach.

"I'm just kidding. Come in, come in," invited Rachel. "Not sure why Hailey still has you outside," she said, flashing her sister a confused look as she rushed to the door. "Welcome to The Sutherland. I'm Rachel, and of course you already know who Hailey is and how she tastes. Can I get you a mojito?"

"A what?" he asked.

Man, he had one sexy voice, Hailey thought. He may have only spoken a few words to her, but that rich baritone was hard to forget. And she'd be strangling her sister later.

"A mojito. Rum, lime, sugar and mint. I'm trying out some recipes. Nothing?" she asked as she ushered him inside and shut the door.

The SEAL shook his head. Actually, to Hailey he *gained* points by not knowing what the drink was. The three of them stood in the foyer, looking at one another. No one said a thing. If she'd thought her apron remark had been awkward…

"Oh, my gosh," Rachel exclaimed, her voice overly bright. "Would you look at the time? It's like, wow, late. Gotta run."

And being extremely obvious in the process. Actually, Hailey wanted her sister and Nate out of here. Okay, not really.

Since Nate was staring at her, Hailey forced herself not to roll her eyes at her sister's comment. Although Hailey had a feeling this man didn't miss much. Rachel had always accused her of becoming like The Terminator when it came to men. She'd automatically run through a list of options and choose which would best annihilate a man's sense of wanting to stay single.

A woman didn't get asked for her hand in marriage without knowing a few things.

With the emo guys, it was music. The brainy type always had a sweet spot for all things techno and gadgety. Her experience didn't run along military lines, but…

She flashed him a small smile. "If you don't mind, I need to finish up a few things in the kitchen. You do like homemade chocolate chip cookies, right?"

He swallowed.

Got him in one.

Hailey suppressed a groan. It could have been so simple: hear what he had to say, turn down anything if he offered, then send him on his way. Male isolation back in full force. But no, she had to let her curiosity take over, and try to find out his weakness.

Back to the bookstore tomorrow. Surely there was something new on impulse control.

And anyway, the fact that he fell so easily to a little cookie manipulation wasn't even sporting. Most men loved anything they didn't have to cook. This man was probably used to that dried powdery stuff you added water to for a meal. Fun on a Girl Scout backyard campout in the third grade, but it'd probably lost its appeal sometime around adulthood.

"I may have some leftover lasagna, too. Actually you'd be doing me a favor by eating it. Leftovers never taste the same to me, and with all the fresh ingredients in the sauce, it would be a shame to leave it wrapped up in the refrigerator." She may have heard him groan.

He silently followed her down the side corridor to the kitchen.

"This is some contrast from the lobby," he said.

She nodded, noting the modern appliances and bright efficient lighting. They'd maintained the Victorian feel of the lobby and foyer that reflected The Sutherland's origin. It still needed a bit more TLC, but she was pretty sure her mother would be pleased. "We take the breakfast part seriously here at The Sutherland B&B, so we needed a good working kitchen. Was that a yes to the lasagna?"

He nodded, and she dished out a healthy serving and

graced the side of the plate with buttered garlic bread. "This was my grandmother's recipe," she said, and she handed him a fork and napkin embroidered with an S.

His eyes closed in appreciation at the first bite. *Thank you grandma.* A man with a full stomach was always easier to deal with. He attacked his food like she assumed he handled life, with focus and determination. He ate while she gathered the ingredients for the cookies. With the former men in her life she would have felt obligated to keep up some kind of running conversation. And despite the fact that her thoughts drifted to that kiss he'd ramped up the heat on more than she cared to admit, she was sticking to her no-men plan, and giving herself a break.

It didn't matter that this guy had an amazing body as evidenced by his skintight wetsuit.

Nope, it wasn't important that he had the most firm, kissable lips she'd ever seen.

And the fact that he had heroic tendencies to throw on top of all that other good stuff, just to ensure she went a little weak in the knees, meant nothing. Hailey was all about self-improvement, and home improvement, if she counted The Sutherland. Men didn't factor into either one of those goals. In fact, men usually interfered with a woman's path to emotional growth.

Hmm, that basecamp food must have been worse than she imagined because he was already done by the time she was rolling little balls of dough. Hailey saved a small amount in the bowl.

"I have a weakness for raw cookie dough. Do you?" she asked.

He nodded and once again she was struck by how

handsome he was. He wore just a plain blue polo shirt matched with a pair of khaki shorts, but she enjoyed observing the strength of his bare arms. Tightly muscled, he didn't have the bulky shape of a body builder, just pure, broad-shouldered strength. It was intimidating.

And thrilling. She was sorely tempted to run her finger along the lines of muscles roping his arms. But those kinds of thoughts led women to playing hide and seek in the sheets.

Hailey pushed the bowl of dough between them, and they both reached inside at the same time, brushing hands. His fingers caught hers, stroked the back of her hand.

"Thank you, Hailey."

She glanced up, way up, and met his eyes. Steely and completely focused on her. The way he said her name, slowing it down in the middle with a hint of something Midwestern was sexy as hell. And then he smiled and she began to wonder if there was an expiration date on her Fate Delivery Card. Like could she kiss him again right now?

"How long have you been a Navy SEAL?" she asked, ready now to fill the air between them with rambling instead of heat.

"Six years," he told her, the smile fading from his lips. "Why'd you kiss me, Hailey?" he asked her quietly. If he hadn't tacked on her name at the end of his question, she could have responded in some glib, flippant way. But how he said her name drew her gaze to his.

"Because I wanted to." And it was true. From the second Nate emerged from the water she hadn't been able to take her eyes off him. His power, confidence and the non-aggrandizing way he took care of his buddy intrigued her.

Fiancé Failure Number Two would have been all about pointing to himself. "Hey, look what I just did. I saved that dude's life."

Yet Nate had calmly taken care of business and when it was over, he was ready to hit the water again.

His gaze settled on her mouth, and she could almost feel the heat of his lips. *Just lean toward him.* That's all she'd have to do, and those lips would be hers once more. No more remembering or imagining a second and a third kiss with him.

But she wouldn't. This was not the right time in her life to be canoodling with men who dropped out of helicopters for a living. When she did start dating, it would be with someone utterly stable. Like an accountant or insurance agent.

The timer dinged announcing that the cookies were ready. *Saved by the bell.* Oh, no, this time she saved herself. Hailey pushed off and away from the counter. Grabbing potholders, she swung open the oven door and pulled out the cookie sheet.

"Glass of milk?" she asked, as she slid the cookies over to the cooling rack.

"Is there any other way to eat cookies?"

With a laugh she opened the refrigerator door. "No, there's not." She poured the glasses of milk and served them two cookies each. As she'd done since she was a child, Hailey tore her cookie, loving the way the melted chocolate chip strung between the two halves.

Nate had already wolfed both his cookies down. "Would you like another?" she asked.

He raised an eyebrow. "What kind of question is that?"

So she served him two more cookies.

The mood had lightened between them.

"Why'd you kiss me? Tell me the real reason this time."

The man knew how to ruin a cookie moment. Suddenly she was back on that beach, feeling his lips take over the kiss she'd started.

"Have you ever heard of Fate Delivery Cards? No, I can see that you haven't. Actually, I have them right here." Hailey walked to the desk in the corner of the kitchen where she and her sister planned the meals for the week for The Sutherland. After grabbing the cards, she handed the packet to Nate.

"Don't wait on fate, jump start your life today." He read off the front of the package. "I always thought you made your own fate."

"Oh, me, too. I just went along with it because it was a party game." Said the woman with fifteen thousand self-help books. "But are you brave enough to take a card?"

"And your card said what? To kiss me?"

She nodded. "Kiss the first man I saw."

"Lucky me," he said, and her breath hitched at the sensual tone of his voice.

"Technically, the hurt guy was the first one I saw, but I didn't think it fair to kiss a defenseless man."

Something flared dark in Nate's eyes. "Feel free to kiss me whenever I'm defenseless."

She doubted this man ever was defenseless. Hailey crossed her arms over her chest, trying to block the attack his words had on her body. He was inviting her to kiss him again. What was that saying? That the best defense was a good offense? "Seems to me you're stalling. You backing down from drawing a card?"

"Oh, I never back down from anything." He made

his statement with straightforward matter-of-fact calmness. Hailey knew he wasn't trying to sound tough for her benefit.

Yeah, she'd bet money he didn't back down. The man jumped out of helicopters.

She pulled the cards from the deck and began to shuffle. Then she fanned the cards out in front of him. "Pick a card, any card," she said, mimicking a magician.

His callused hand rested on hers instead of the cards she offered.

"Go out on a date with me," he urged.

She wrinkled her nose. "I don't do relationships."

"Good. I don't do them either," he said, drawing a card from the ones she held.

Which begged the question…why not? Nate glanced down at the card and read. A smile tugged at the corner of his mouth.

"What does it say?" she asked, overwhelmed by curiosity.

He stood. "I'll bring the card with me when I pick you up Saturday morning."

A week away. Her heart pounded, and she realized she was enjoying the byplay between them. "I haven't said yes yet." She followed him out of the kitchen into the foyer. *No no no.* That *yet* just stole away how cool she wanted to play this.

Nate looked over his shoulder and shot her the sexiest look a man had ever given a woman. "Ten."

Hailey couldn't believe she was nodding. "Okay." Man, she'd really lost control of that one.

He bent and placed a quick kiss to her unsuspecting, but very appreciative lips. Before she could say anything, he closed the door behind him. Hailey leaned against the wall, hugging the cards to her chest. She knew she wore a goofy smile.

NATE WHISTLED AS HE readied his H-gear for the next day. When had he ever whistled? If anything, the Navy had taught him to be even more silent than was his natural affinity for it. And here he was, whistling all the same. And he knew the cause.

Hailey Sutherland.

The woman was even more beautiful this evening. With her hair in a messy knot on the top of her head as she'd easily made him cookies, he'd never seen a woman as sexy. He didn't know which he wanted more, the woman or the cookie. Actually, that wasn't true. The woman. However, the cookie was the prudent choice.

He hadn't any intention of asking her out tonight— he merely wanted an explanation about the kiss. Soon he'd be back up to a hundred percent and deployed, and like a lot of career SEALs, his line of work and women didn't always mesh.

But when she told him she didn't do relationships, it sounded a little too much like a challenge. Did he secretly want her to consider a relationship with him? Not that he wanted one.

Nate carefully inspected and attached his radio and medical kit to the standard issue H-harness. Tomorrow he'd demonstrate to the men how to get first, second and third line gear ready. They didn't know it yet, but then the trainees would be cut loose for some land nav exercises. He smiled in anticipation. The fun part.

He made quick work of his equipment. This was the easy part, and he'd been doing it so long he could do it without thinking. Unlike how he ended up with a date with the lady from the B&B. He'd had to put a lot of effort into that because Nate felt out of his element with Hailey, a situation he'd never found himself in before, and was irritated by it.

She wasn't like the women he usually spent his off-duty time with, women who knew what they were getting with the kind of man who liked playing sports, drinking a beer and keeping it casual.

Although the woman claimed she didn't do relationships, nothing about Hailey seemed casual. She glided around in a flowery dress with a ruffle at the bottom that drew his eyes to her great legs. She wore heels, and her toenails were painted a sexy bright pink.

This wouldn't be a bowling date. There wouldn't be an evening at the batting cages or catching the Chargers practice. With Hailey, he might have to wear a tie.

But then she may take it off. A more than fair tradeoff.

Why had he made their date so many days away? Since that afternoon on the beach he couldn't stop his thoughts straying to her sweet smile and concerned hazel eyes. If he'd made the date tomorrow he wouldn't have to think about how much he enjoyed talking to her as she bustled around in the kitchen. Or imagine what her lips would taste like if he were involved right from the beginning.

And he definitely wouldn't have to keep wondering about her reaction when she saw the suggestion on his Fate Delivery Card…and whether or not she'd deliver on it?

A SOFT RAP SOUNDED on her bedroom door, and Hailey scooted up against the pillows, tossing her book aside. "Come in," she called.

Rachel poked her head around the door. "Glad you weren't already sleeping."

Hailey shook her head. "I was just laying here."

With a smile, Rachel walked in and plopped herself on the pillows. Her sister had been plopping herself down on Hailey's bed since she could remember. Over the years and side by side, they'd played Barbies, talked about boys and made plans long into the night, or at least until their parents told them to knock it off.

She knew her sister was here for a play-by-play of her encounter with Nate.

"Did you leave any dough for me?" she asked.

Hailey laughed. They both had a weakness for the raw stuff. "In a leftover butter dish in the back of the fridge."

"Thanks. And don't think just because you left me some that I will be forgetting that you made the man cookies. Cookies. Bringing out the big guns right from the beginning? Didn't Mom caution about using her secret weapon too early?" she asked with a brow raised.

"Just to soften the blow for when I told him no about seeing him again."

"Ha. So when are you going out?" Rachel asked.

"Saturday. How did you know?"

"Nate looks like the kind of guy who gets what he wants, and big sis, that man wants you. Bad."

Every part of Hailey began to tingle. *This* was why she needed male isolation. Tingles equaled bad decisions. "You know, I've been thinking about that Navy SEAL."

Rachel's eyes grew wide. "Of course you have, I

knew it wasn't one-sided. That kitchen was about twenty degrees hotter after he left, and it didn't have anything to do with you baking cookies."

"Actually, I wasn't thinking of him *that* way," Hailey admonished. *Liar.* She wasn't thinking of him *that* way at *that* moment. "Do you remember how excited all those women got when the SEALs began climbing down that rope?"

"One practically knocked me over getting to the railing."

"Exactly. No one could take their eyes off them, and that was before the one got injured. I say, give the women what they want."

Rachel's head cocked to one side, the sure sign she was intrigued. "Tell me more."

"I'm thinking bistro stools and tables out on the terrace. We'd serve some of the finger food that The Sutherland used to serve at brunch."

"Maybe update it a bit, mojitos and champagne iced tea," Rachel suggested, clearly warming to the idea. Food was her specialty. "And then what, we just wait for the SEALs to show up?"

Sucking in her bottom lip, Hailey thought that could be too tricky, since she knew now from first-hand experience that SEALs could be a bit unpredictable, although she hadn't noticed they followed any set schedule. "We'll bill it as a party night. We'll play Texas Hold 'Em."

Rachel's expression turned questioning.

"Non-gambling poker, of course. Or that new game everyone likes, Bunco. The SEALs would be an added bonus."

"But we'd all know we were there for the SEALs,"

Rachel added, smiling. "I think this could actually work. We can offer a special reduced rate on the rooms during the weeknights since we're slower than on Fridays and Saturdays. We'd be out the expense of the terrace furniture, but eventually better off with the additional money coming in."

"SEAL night it is."

4

AIR WEEK FOR HIS TRAINEES was almost over. They'd begin land navigation next, Nate's specialty. Although with his bum leg, he'd need extra help to run the drills. He hated feeling like he couldn't take care of business.

Today they'd be practicing a Rubber Duck insertion. Men on The Teams performed this with ease, and so must these SEAL trainees.

Nate observed closely as his trainees pushed out their duck, or inflated rubber boat, now outfitted with large cargo parachutes. Then the trainees jumped from the plane quickly behind the duck. Soon parachutes filled the sky.

Now it was Nate's turn. As a SEAL, he felt most comfortable in the water, but there was something about free falling, before the jerk of the cord and the abrupt halt of descent, that was exhilarating. Like a fine whisky, or riding with the top down, even making love to a beautiful woman, the anticipation was every bit as good as the experience.

His thoughts conjured Hailey's lovely face. The parting of her lips after he'd kissed her. The joy of sinking his hands into her hair. Pulling her close without an audience.

Nate jumped.

The rubber ducks, or inflatable rafts, allowed them to cover more area and carry more gear than a fast line descent into the water, and already the trainees were taking care of business as they'd done over and over in the classroom.

In a flash, he was in the water, his body ready for the shock, although SEALs weren't strangers to being wet and cold. That was pretty much his status quo during BUD/S Hell Week. Even after obtaining his Trident, and becoming an official SEAL, he'd spent some quality time in the Alaskan glacier-fed waters of Chiniak Bay. The water here off the coast of California was about fifty-two degrees—what most SEALs called toasty warm.

"They're here, ladies!" was his welcome as he broke the surface of the water. Followed by…female catcalls?

Nate pivoted to face the beach and spotted about nine women waving and calling to him and his men. One carried a bullhorn. "Look at them getting into the boat," she said, and the others cheered.

He looked over, and sure enough, two SEAL trainees were hoisting themselves over the sides of the rubber boat with a minimum of effort.

Had these women been waiting for them? Nate couldn't believe it. One woman carried a sign that had what must be a phone number. All held martini glasses. Two more SEALs were approaching the boat to more cheers and catcalls.

"619-4—"

"Ensign." Nate's harsh tone cut the remaining phone number recitation. In irritation he turned toward the women. Didn't they understand these men were conducting training that might save their asses one day?

The ladies stood in the approximate area where he'd received the hottest, most surprising kiss of his life. That couldn't be an accident. He scanned the women mingling near the water, but did not see her. Where was Hailey? He'd recognize that body anywhere. He tamped down the inappropriate surge of disappointment.

Maybe she was working. His gaze switched to the large hotel, which stood several hundred yards behind the women.

And he spotted her. He sucked in a breath as his eyes alighted on her beautiful bare legs. He followed the smooth line of her thighs, interrupted by khaki colored shorts. Her midriff was also bare, and his fingers curved in the water in the same way as he ached to shape his hands around her waist. He suppressed a groan as his gaze traveled over her small, shapely breasts. Breasts he'd felt pressed against his chest and thought about as he lay in his bunk alone at night.

She lounged on one of the recliners, wearing large sunglasses and her beautiful light brown sandy-colored hair loose about her shoulders. Her lips arced in an inviting smile, and he almost returned one of his own. Then she lifted her drink glass in greeting and he knew. She was the person responsible for the shenanigans out there on the beach.

"Smile for the cameras, boys," one of the women called.

Out of the corner of his eye he spotted another one of his men wave.

"What the hell are you doing?" Nate demanded.

"Representing the U.S. Navy, sir."

Letting them off easy in the weight room had been a mistake. "Look," another one of his men said.

A woman lifted her top and flashed his men something they'd been missing for weeks due to training. Okay, he was pulling the plug on this. Order was disappearing. He'd planned for a slow drift through the water for the men to practice their patient silent approach. Now they'd be working on speed, and getting back to the base as quickly as possible.

Yeah, back at the base where he'd plan an attack of a different kind. He and Hailey had some business to discuss.

HAILEY WATCHED THE MEN in their boats until they were just tiny dots in the ocean. She needed someplace cool and she needed it now. Hailey felt hot and achy and restless. Her cheeks were flushed, and even where her clothes touched skin felt uncomfortable.

The commercial icemaker would do the trick. A few fell into her hand from the dispenser and she ran the cube along the back of her neck, then across her chest.

"Is it really that hot out there?" Rachel asked.

The ice dropped from her hand and fell to the floor. Hailey hadn't even realized her sister was in the kitchen. "I, uh, um…"

"Never mind. I know what that's all about. Well, you keep having your male-induced panic attack. Meanwhile, the women are calling for more mojitos," Rachel said, as she mixed limejuice and rum together in a pitcher.

"You saw that outside, right?"

"That display of capable male hotness?"

"Yes," she said, her breath came out in a rush. "They jumped out of a plane, Rachel! That's like the sexiest thing I've ever seen."

"Woo hoo, Hailey's living again. This calls for a drink," Rachel said as she poured herself a small glass of the mojito.

"What are you talking about?" Hailey asked, feeling defensive. This wasn't the first time her sister had implied she wasn't herself. Didn't her sister know that was exactly what she was trying to do? Remember who she was?

"You've been focused on nothing but getting The Sutherland back into shape and self-improvement for the last four months."

"Both of them need some work," Hailey responded drily.

"Maybe a little, but sis, you've taken it overboard. Completely distancing yourself from men, what's with that?"

This was unfair. "I'm resetting my inner attraction switch. It's outlined perfectly in *Stop Picking the Wrong Men*. That book really opened my eyes to my own destructive dating patterns. Cutting out men from my life has really worked out great. I can begin Step Two at the end of the month."

"I'm afraid to ask what that entails."

"It's dating myself. Relearning me. Who I am, what I want, what I'm attracted to."

"I think your body is telling you what you're attracted to."

"That's pure animal attraction," Hailey said with a brush of her hand. "I mean, what woman wouldn't be attracted to big broad shoulders and a tight hard body? Or that great smile of his? And Nate's gray eyes. When he looked at me all hot and…" Hailey sunk her head into her hands. "Ohmygod, you're right. I want him."

Rachel gave her a sympathetic squeeze to her shoulder. "It's not so bad. Listen, I'm going to give you the outline of my latest, Why Hailey Chooses Dumb Moves."

Hailey lifted her gaze. "I thought you told me it wasn't going to be so bad. You just called me dumb."

"I called your choices dumb. Let me keep going. You grew up watching mom and dad and their great relationship, and knew you wanted the same thing."

"How do you know so much about what I want?"

Her sister's expression turned ironic. "Because, honey, I have the same problem. It's just manifested itself in a different way. I became a waiter—waiting for Mr. Perfect, whereas you became a fixer. Take your first fiancé, the emo guy."

"Adam? He had such talent. What a painter, remember?"

"I remember you buying a lot of canvas and very expensive paints. He never seemed to have the money for the essentials of his trade, but he had a lot of dreams and not many plans."

"That was simply his artistic nature," she said, shrugging.

"So you planned it all, and worked so hard to make everything come out perfect, and hide all the problems so he wouldn't be so down all the time. So when that fizzled you went with the complete opposite. Mr. Efficient, businessman."

"Mason."

Rachel made a face. "I'd almost forgotten that controlling bastard's name. At least you had something in common with the last one—you both were in love with him."

Hailey rubbed the back of her neck, trying to prevent a knot wanting to form. "What's the point of bringing all this up? I'm trying to fix my life now."

"But honey, that's just it. The fixer in you is the problem. It's why you have a thousand self-help books upstairs in your room, but wind up at the same place every time."

"So how do I stop attempting to fix everything?"

Rachel flashed her a wry smile. "I know the problem, but I don't have the solution. That one you will have to figure out all on your own." Then after tossing in a few fresh mint leaves, Rachel slid the pitcher of mojitos across the granite countertop toward her sister. "But right now, Hailey, you can deliver more drinks. I think I hear the ladies out there getting restless since the SEALs are gone."

"This worked better than I thought it would, and we did this in under two days. Imagine what we could do with more than just phone calls and a few flyers."

"Amy really came through for us. We wouldn't have had nearly that kind of response if she hadn't gotten on the horn and invited her friends."

"Does she seem the same to you?" Rachel asked. "She seems more…subdued almost. I noticed it after the bridal party when we were loading her car with the gifts. I thought maybe she was tired, but today she seems even worse."

"Are those mojitos ready?" Amy asked as she pushed her way into the kitchen.

"Were your ears burning? We were just talking about you," Hailey said.

"Better be good things," Amy warned with a slight smile.

"You seem…not yourself," Rachel said.

"Don't worry. Rachel accuses everyone of that lately," Hailey teased as she picked up a dishtowel.

Amy shrugged. "No, everything's fine."

The two sisters looked at each other. Okay, maybe Rachel *was* onto something. Women excited about getting married didn't look mopey and tell everyone she was fine. Hailey should know, she had this engagement thing down pat. "You sure?" Hailey questioned.

Amy plastered a tight smile across her face. "Absolutely."

"We didn't mean to put you to work," Rachel said. "But as long as you are, how are we on the finger foods?" she asked.

"We're good," Amy said, laughing. "I'm heading out."

Once Amy had left the kitchen, Rachel blurted, "See what I'm talking about? Something seems off with her."

The doorbell rang. All this use, and still it sounded terrible. "I'll get it," her sister said, and headed toward the lobby.

Hailey put the dishtowel to use and began to wipe up the water some of the crushed ice had left behind. She'd always hated The Sutherland growing up, rejected the idea that she'd ever take her place behind the counter, making beds, preparing food and welcoming people. Okay, hate was a strong word. She just hadn't wanted this life, it hadn't seemed exciting to a fifteen-year-old wanting to travel the world and see everything.

But that fifteen-year-old hadn't yet had her heart broken. Three times. Hadn't realized the comfort of being surrounded by family, in a familiar place.

With a not so discreet clearing of her throat, Rachel announced her return. And there was a guest in tow.

Nate Peterson.

Unlike last time, the man didn't appear too happy about his visit to The Sutherland. However, his stern and tired expression only made him all the more appealing. She wanted to stroke the tension from him. Hailey's stomach did a little flutter. Now that she'd acknowledged how much she desired him, she didn't feel as bold as when they stood together on the beach. The idea of walking over to him and stealing a kiss filled her with shivers, not resolve.

"I guess I'll go check on the party, sounds like it's winding down," Rachel said as she exited.

Good Lord, there was the tunnel vision *Stop Picking the Wrong Men* warned about. Hailey hadn't even remembered her sister was in the room. Laughter drifted in from the other room.

"Actually, your guests are what I wanted to discuss with you," he said after dragging his gaze from her lips.

Yes. He felt it, too.

Except she had a suspicion this little discussion wasn't going to be pleasant.

Hailey had this handled. Would Nate like peanut butter cookies as much as chocolate chip? The man had definitely responded to the whole warm kitchen feeling of a few nights ago. Maybe she should work on writing a book on drawing a man's attention away from a problem. Why did women always find it so difficult dealing with men? Food and sex, sometimes they camouflaged most anything. Now, to find that peanut butter…

What was it her sister had said? That Hailey worked so hard to hide all the problems? That's certainly what she was doing now. She swallowed. Hailey could follow the same pattern she'd used with every other man in her life, or she could try something new.

She took a deep breath. Hailey met his gaze, instead of opening the cabinet for the peanut butter. She was done smoothing things over.

Nate leaned forward, balancing on the center island separating them. The sturdy muscles of his arms flexed as he moved, and once again she was taken in by his amazing physical side. Everything about him seemed to suggest leashed danger.

"So what happened on the beach this afternoon, that was a one-time occurrence, right?" he asked.

Hailey folded her arms across her chest. "Not so sure about that," she drawled, as if it was a standoff from the Old West.

He reached into his pocket and pulled out a neatly folded piece of paper. "You're done with these flyers, too." Nate spread out the flyer they'd quickly put together at the local copy shop announcing Spot A SEAL day at The Sutherland.

"We just made those yesterday. How did you find one so fast?"

"The U.S. Navy has excellent intel."

A little mojito would be great right about now. She sighed, blowing the wisp of her bangs. "Okay, how bad is this?"

"That depends," he said, his glance straying once more to her mouth.

"On what?"

Then that gray gaze of his slammed right into hers. "On how bad do you want it to be?"

5

NATE WOULD HAVE LAUGHED at Hailey's widened eyes if she didn't look so cute. Or so damn sexy. A slight flush began to spread down her neck and across her collarbone. The exact same path he'd take with his mouth. His tongue.

Hailey wanted him. She wanted him every bit as badly as he wanted her. His body tightened in response.

With a rueful shake of her head, Hailey reached for the handle of one of the cabinets. Cookies? His mouth began to water. Then a dozen possibilities filled his vision. Eating that cookie off Hailey's stomach was his favorite.

To his disappointment, she reached for a pitcher. "We need some more mojitos."

"I thought the party was winding down."

She sucked in the corner of her full bottom lip. Sexy as hell. "This one's for me," she told him.

He watched as she gathered fresh limes, sugar, rum and some sort of leafy thing that looked like raw spinach.

"I love the smell of fresh mint," she said.

That explained the green leafy thing.

She gently bent the leaf and held it to his nose. "Smell," she urged.

Nate reached for her wrist and drew her closer to

him. He breathed in the scent, never taking his eyes off her face. Hailey's skin was softer than anything he'd ever touched. Her breath hitched as he drew her closer still.

Hailey's other hand fluttered to his shoulder, her fingers curled into his shirt. He groaned and dropped her wrist and cupped her face. He didn't need to draw her lips to his. She met him, her lips easily willing against his.

The rush he felt when she traced his bottom lip with her tongue equaled that of fast lining out of a helicopter. He needed her. Now.

Hailey used the hand draped around his shoulder to push herself away. She turned her back to him, her chest raising and lowering as she drew in deep gulps of air. He thought he may have heard her mumble stop, "picking the wrong men," but his thinking must be muddled from that kiss she'd laid on him

She spun on her heel. "I'm so sorry."

"Wh-what?"

Hailey nervously wrung her hands. "I hope you don't think I kissed you just now to try to make you forget why you were here."

Kissing Hailey *was* why he was here.

She lowered her hands to her sides. "Nate, you look like the kind of man who appreciates a straight answer, so I'm going to give it to you. This was only our first beach party, and we brought in several hundred dollars. We recently rescued our family home from a management company determined to let it fail, and I busted my 401k on everything you see in the kitchen. You and the rest of the SEALs have already brought in money with a minimum of effort on our part and none on yours.

Each one of those women paid a cover charge. The next time there will be room bookings."

"Those men are in training." He gently traced her lower lip. "I'm sure I don't have to tell you how distracting a woman can be."

"How about if I put a stop to the signage and flashing?" she asked, and his stomach clenched at the hopeful tone in her voice.

This was why relationships were hard. Hailey needed the money, he knew it, and still he was going to ask her to stop. "Those aren't just games they're playing out there. They're learning how to protect themselves and to keep *you* safe."

"Maybe you could give me a schedule of your less dangerous exercises and we could work around that."

"They're all dangerous."

She slumped against the counter. "The money is just so good," she said, not even attempting to hide the disappointment in her voice.

He wanted to help. This woman had nearly made him senseless with a kiss grounded firmly in PG on the movie rating scale, tempted him with cookies, and now she triggered all kinds of protective urges. Looking into her hazel eyes, Nate admitted, "We can't make you stop, it's a free beach…"

She perked up immediately.

"*I'm* just asking you to do the right thing here."

Her shoulders slumped. He could fight his newfound desire to comfort or he could roll with it. Nate drew her forward, and Hailey didn't resist as she moved into his arms, warm and fitting perfectly against his side. Rolling with it…definitely the right way to go. "I know you will come up with something," he whispered against her hair. "Maybe we can think of something together on our date."

Hailey pulled away, and blinked up into his eyes. "Together? As in we come up with ideas…" Her voice trailed off.

Nate nodded. "Together."

Her jaw angled to the right. "You don't want me to fix this problem all on my own?"

"Why would I want you to do that?" As a SEAL Team, they repeatedly went over every detail of a dive together, ferreting out weaknesses, looking for ways to improve. It only made sense. What kind of man wouldn't do the same with a woman he wanted to help?

Her eyes softened, and Nate remembered his original intention in tugging Hailey close—to roll with it. He'd meant for the kiss to be gentle. Soothing. But as soon as his lips brushed hers, Hailey sunk her fingers into his hair and pressed herself against him. The tips of her breasts brushed his chest, and all he could think was heaven. And more.

The woman knew how to kiss. And that was his last thought before hunger for this sexy woman took over. Her hands moved up and down his back, and she hooked a leg over his thigh creating the perfect cradle for his growing erection. Hailey was a small woman, but her breasts filled his hands as if they were meant to be there. He groaned as he felt her nipples harden through the material of her bra and blouse.

She broke away from their kiss, and nibbled on his neck, then the lobe of his ear. Her soft sigh as his hand slipped under her shirt to stroke the bare skin of her stomach nearly did him in. Deployment and injury had kept him celibate long enough.

Then his knee gave out.

He groaned at the sharp pain attacking his joint.

Hailey's movements abruptly stopped. Her leg slid down to the floor. "That wasn't a good kind of groan, was it?" she asked, concern lacing his voice.

Nate squeezed his eyes tight, willing his thigh muscles to relax. But he wasn't in so much agony that he didn't miss her worried tone. The little massaging motions of her hands on his shoulders only confirmed her apprehension. Opening his eyes, he cupped her face and smiled. "Not a good kind of groan."

Now he could add one more label to the injury that took him off the Teams. Mood killer.

"What happened?" she asked.

He reached for her hand and she immediately twined her fingers through his. "It's not the most romantic of stories."

Hailey made a scoffing sound. "Don't worry, I'm not the romantic type."

"Not falling for it," he told her, making his way through the kitchen toward the door that led to the lobby, Hailey's soft hand still snug in his. "They may not want to admit it, but deep down, all women want romance."

"Believe me, that's so not true," she said, rolling her eyes.

"That sounds a lot like a challenge."

She held both hands up in surrender. "No, no challenge, it's a lost cause. I hate flowers, don't even think about stuffed animals, and never, *never* mix me a CD of cheesy love songs."

"I never think about stuffed animals."

"I just prefer deeds over gestures," she told him, and he got the feeling this woman had received plenty of talk but not a lot of substance.

They passed the stairs together. Did those stairs lead up to her bedroom? Hell, it was a B&B, the place was filled with beds. If he asked, would she take him upstairs?

Something hot burned between them, there was no denying it, but did he want to hound dog his way through life? He knew two minutes out the door, he'd regret not having her in his arms again. In ten minutes he'd want to kick his own ass. Being a SEAL had taught him patience; nearly getting killed had forced him to take life slower. Strange, he'd even missed the party tonight, and didn't care.

It wasn't so long ago that if a woman told him she didn't want a relationship he would have cheered. But with Hailey...she was the kind of woman to relish. To savor.

Nate forced his eyes off the tempting stairs and reached for the doorknob instead.

Hailey might not have realized it, but she revealed something to him tonight, something vulnerable. He sensed she wasn't the kind of woman who did that often. She'd already told him she didn't do relationships, now she was down on romance.

Nate wanted to change that.

"You didn't show me your card," she told him as he stepped into the cool night air.

"That's right," he replied, then quietly closed the door behind him.

AMY BRADFORD HAD A fire to start, and it was going to be a big one. Accidentally barging in on Hailey practically crawling on the SEAL in the kitchen had, well, sealed the deal so to speak.

She wanted *that*.

That passion, that hunger for another person so consuming neither even noticed that someone had walked in on you while in each other's arms.

Yearning for passion should probably not be on the wish list of a woman about to be married in a few days. She should already have the passion. Be looking forward to making that passion permanent.

Which was why she needed the fire. A fire so big the shuttle would be able to spot it from space. Hmm, maybe the backyard wasn't such a good idea. Neighbors tended to make phone calls. She quickly cleared the area around her sink, moving the dirty cups and spoons to a dishtowel. This cluttered area would just have to do, there was no time to get them clean and put away.

Her skirt swished around her knees as she opened and slammed drawers looking for a lighter or some forgotten book of matches. There were none. Desperate, she glanced down at the ruffle of her sundress. Okay, cool spring cotton with pastel flowers that she'd worn to the Spot the Seal party didn't seem appropriate for building an inferno.

Calm down.

She took a deep breath. Thought of the ocean. A bubble bath. Hot chocolate. *Control the panic. Make it subside.* Her heartbeat slowed, and now she could actually think.

Be smart about this.

Amy reached above her head and pulled down a glass to fill with tap water. After draining the contents, she placed it upside down on the dishtowel already filled with the dirty dishes from her sink. Her hand was shaking, but growing steadier. *Good.* Her cell phone rang, the special ringtone telling her it was Jake on the line.

A tiny prickle of the panic returned.

Jake Arkins, her fiancé, the love of her life, the man she had to avoid pronto. "Hello," she answered.

"Hey, I thought you were going to tell me what time to meet you back at our place," he said. His voice was a deep baritone that never failed to send shivers down her back. "Our place, that has a nice ring to it."

It did until that card. Now "our place" sounded a lot like "lack of privacy." "Mmmm," she managed as a response.

"How'd the party go?" he asked.

She nodded before she answered. "Good, good. We all had a good time," she said, her gaze examining each closed cabinet, as she tried to remember if a box of matches could be behind the door. Earlier this week, she'd sorted through every drawer and every cabinet combining her stuff with his. Now her mind was a blank.

"Thought maybe you could show off some of that naughty lingerie you got from the shower before dinner."

She'd need the fire extinguisher, too. She'd had the thing so long maybe it had expired. Did fire extinguishers go bad?

"Amy?" Jake asked, his voice uncertain.

Oh, hell, what had he asked? Dinner? "Yeah, I have it all in the crock-pot."

Jake chuckled. "Sounds sexy."

Under the kitchen sink. That's where they'd stashed

the extinguisher. She lowered to her knees and began to rustle through the cleaning supplies. Wait, a crockpot sounded sexy?

How could she forget? They'd made plans to hide out at their duplex and not worry about wedding details for the rest of the evening, and just be together.

Except she didn't have time for sexy right now. Although she yearned to have his strong arms around her. He always made her feel safe from the outside world.

Amy gave herself a quick mental shake. *Task at hand.* "Jake, I'm sorry I didn't call. With this party tonight and all the wedding details, I'm a little distracted."

"Ames, it's okay. You sound pretty stressed. I'm on my way home now, and we'll unplug the phones and I'll take your mind off of fittings and flowers and whatever else it is your grandma says a wedding must have."

The heat of his words and the promise in his voice made her heart pound again. For all the wrong reasons. "If I don't start cracking on these thank you notes, my grandmother will never forgive me. You know how she is about etiquette." And she had a fire to start, to put out and hide all the evidence.

"I love you," he said.

She closed her eyes, allowing herself to really feel the emotion. How had she been so lucky to find a man like Jake who loved her in return? Fate had really smiled—

Fate.

Her stomach clenched and all the warm feelings of just a moment ago vanished. "I love you, too," she said over the lump in her throat. Amy closed the phone and returned it to her purse. Something else was tucked there. The stupid Fate Delivery Card she'd been forced to take. The thing she'd been avoiding but had gotten her into this mess in the first place.

After the excitement of Hailey's kiss on the beach with the hot Navy SEAL everyone had forgotten that she'd drawn a card. It wasn't until she stopped off to get a soft drink at the drive thru that she'd found the Fate Delivery Card she'd stuffed in her purse.

With a smile, she remembered the hilarious things Tori and Hailey had to complete. What did fate have in store for her? In excited anticipation she'd turned the card over and read.

Amy wasn't smiling now. Her fingers crumpled the plastic coated card as she yanked the hated thing once more from her purse. She would read it again. Not that the last seven times she'd read it had changed the very clear message.

Set something you love free.

Its challenge was clear. Jake. Amy was supposed to set Jake free.

And that's why she was going to set that sucker on fire—pretending the card had never happened hadn't worked. She'd practically taken a second job at The Sutherland to avoid going home. Amy knew it seemed irrational, but it made some weird kind of sense that if she could just remove any trace that the card had ever existed, everything would go back to normal. No harm, no foul.

Except she couldn't find anything to use as a lighter. Jake was allergic to scented candles, there wasn't a fireplace in the new home and the stove was electric, not gas.

She was screwed.

Or maybe fate was telling her something. She slumped to the floor with her back against the stainless steel of the refrigerator door. She loved Jake, she really did…but something wasn't right. It had niggled her for weeks, months, and now, when she couldn't destroy the one thing that was trying to shed light on the problem she'd been hoping to ignore, Amy had to face it. All thanks to that stupid, stupid card. She buried her face in her hands for a moment, but no tears would come.

Only resolve.

Amy stood up, kicked off her pretty strappy sandals, and padded barefoot on the travertine flooring she and Jake had installed together not long ago. In the bedroom, one of her suitcases lay on its side. She'd only unpacked it two days ago. Quickly tossing it on the bed. She unzipped the top, and in a daze began to pack.

Where would she go? Her reasoning was too stupid to try and explain it to her grandparents. Besides, her grandma would be the last person to understand. Her old roommate already had someone moved into Amy's old bedroom.

But as she zipped her suitcase shut, she knew here was only one place to go.

"I CHECKED THE DOORS and set the alarm. The Sutherland is officially closed for the night," Hailey said, as she slumped next to Rachel on one of the rosewood couches in the lobby, newly reupholstered in a deep burgundy. The sisters had completed the work themselves, tackling one a week so the lobby wouldn't be bare for their guests. The sitting area could still use a bit of refreshing to its Victorian décor, but they could look at the condition of their childhood home with some pride.

"We keep having nights like tonight, we can buy

some new silk lampshades and fund the electrical wiring for that wall sconce idea you had." This area had originally been illuminated by candles along the perimeter, but when the house was wired for electricity, that charming Victorian detail had been lost. Faux electrical candle lights would do the trick.

But Hailey's stomach tensed at the mention of money. She hated the idea of disappointing her sister. Or Nate.

"Although we should probably hire someone to help with the serving," Rachel continued, "we won't be able to count on Amy, especially after she gets married."

Hailey nodded. "Yeah, I'm surprised she even showed up and stayed that long. Although I've never actually been a bride I've seen those to do lists in bridal magazines. It's brutal."

"Which is why I think something is going on with her and Jake." Her sister sat up, fully alert. "Speaking of relationships, what happened between you and the SEAL? I can't believe I forgot to ask."

"Right. I'm surprised you didn't pounce on me earlier."

"I'm going to blame it on the mojito." Rachel closed her eyes once more. "And don't think you're going to misdirect my attention so you don't have to answer the question. You can't fool me like you once did."

The good old days for sure. As the youngest, Rachel had always been so gullible and easy to manage.

"He came to talk to me about watching the SEALs."

Rachel's eyes snapped open a second time. "That's great. Maybe on your date you can fish around for when the SEALs will be training again. We could put actual times on our flyers."

"Actually, I wanted to talk to you about the party. He didn't like it."

Rachel's eyes narrowed. "Don't tell me. He convinced you to stop our SEAL watch party."

Hailey began to squirm. "I didn't exactly tell him we wouldn't do the parties again, but he did raise some good points."

"Which means we're not having the parties. I'd actually be impressed by his negotiation skills if I weren't irritated that we'll be out all that green. How'd he do it?"

"He appealed to my sense of duty, and how the women are distracting to the men while they were training."

"Sucker."

Probably. For the man. His argument and his grey eyes. Her lips still tingled. "Don't worry, I thought of another idea. Don't you have a friend who works at the San Diego Visitors' Bureau? Well, I'm going to need that number."

"This sound intriguing. I thi—" The rusty sound of the doorbell cut off Rachel's idea.

"We've got to get that fixed. Who'd be ringing now? All the guests are accounted for."

The bell sounded again.

"Whoever it is, they don't seem to be leaving. Better see who it is." Hailey quickly made her way to the large wooden front door that had welcomed hundreds of guests through the decades.

Hailey peered through the peephole. "It's Amy."

"Weird. Maybe she left something."

"We should probably just give you a key," Rachel said.

Their friend and happy bride appeared to be anything but. Her cheeks were blotchy, but a firmness lay across her chin.

"Oh, Amy, what happened?" Hailey asked.

"That stupid card of yours, *that's* what happened." Amy thrust the card at Hailey, then reached for a large suitcase which she rolled into the foyer.

"What are you doing?" Rachel asked.

Hailey was already turning over the card, a tight knot of dread growing in her chest. "Set something you love free," she read aloud. Damn, it was worse than she could have imagined.

Rachel gasped, then jumped up and curved her arm around Amy's shoulder. "Sweetie, it was just silly game. It didn't mean anything."

"I said that to myself the whole drive home. Then every day since. You want to know what happened today? Nothing. I tried to burn the stupid card but I couldn't find one thing to catch it on fire. I can't believe I let Jake talk me out of gas burners for the new range."

The two sisters looked at each other. Clearly they had a case of wedding jitters gone bad on their hands. It might not be in the job description of B&B owner, but surely friends could talk one overwrought bride into calming down. Rachel made a slight nod toward the kitchen.

"Follow me and we'll get you some warm tea and figure this out," Hailey said, as she touched Amy's elbow to direct her. A cup of chamomile tea had always been their mother's remedy, and Hailey fell back on it now. The soft warm brew soothed as well as encouraged talking.

Amy allowed herself to be led a few feet. "I don't even have a lighter in my car. Just an outlet to plug in electronics. Is that insane or what?"

Rachel opened the kitchen door. "Well, listen, if burning is the problem, don't worry about it. Plenty of matches in this place, and our range has eight burners. Each one of them gas."

Amy slumped into one of the chairs at the country style butcher-block table. "I appreciate it, but not being able to burn the card was just the tip-off. Maybe fate has been trying to clue me in all along. There's something fundamentally wrong in my relationship with Jake, and maybe taking seven days away from the wedding planning and the new place will be good for me."

Hailey had been down this road before. She'd aim for soothing tones. "Take it from a woman who has been engaged three times. Once you start thinking a break's a good idea, it soon becomes a reality. Jake probably doesn't even realize you're gone. You can head over there now."

Amy flashed her a tight smile, her face determined. "Oh, I'm not going. The card said set him free, and that's what I'm doing. I'm staying here."

Both sisters began talking at once.

"Oh, but—"

"We don't—"

"I'll pay you," Amy said.

Ahhh, those sweet, magic words.

"Welcome to The Sutherland," Rachel told her.

Hailey shot her sister a fierce look. "She's kidding. We don't want your money." The kettle began to whistle. "You drink your tea while I look at the register for an open room." She fled to the check-in area, and ran her finger down the computer screen. Having the party that afternoon, they'd skipped cleaning their newly-vacated rooms in order to take care of decorating the terrace and making sure it was in tiptop shape.

It had saved time, but now it severely limited which spaces were available. They had one room left. The bridal suite.

Hailey placed an "X" next to the room number and grabbed the key.

Fate did indeed have an ironic sense of humor.

6

NATE HAD NEVER BEEN a dinner and movie kind of guy, but he suspected that's the kind of date Hailey was used to. He avoided his natural inclination toward the water fun of San Diego. Although he would have loved to explore the tidepools at Point Loma or even surf, none of those seemed romantic. And that was his goal here today, lots and lots of romance.

He'd told Hailey to dress casually, and to wear good walking shoes. He could tell by the long pause on the phone she was surprised, but he didn't believe in retreat. He'd see these plans through, and once he'd had more of an opportunity to observe Hailey, he'd choose something better suited to her interests next time.

She opened the door for him quickly, not making him wait. He liked that. Dressed in jeans to her knees, white tennis shoes, casual pink polo shirt and her wavy hair in a high ponytail at the top of her head, Nate didn't regret the casual approach. Hailey looked sexy as hell, and when she flashed him a welcoming smile he couldn't help smiling back.

"I'm ready," she said. She held up a white sack with pink polka dots. "I even made some peanut butter cookies."

"You know how to keep a man coming around, don't you? But why don't you show me your place before we leave."

Her eyes widened in surprise. "You sure?"

"We're not on any kind of schedule."

"You weren't kidding when you said casual."

"My whole life is a schedule, so when I'm off it, I don't even want to see a clock."

"Duly noted." She reached around and closed the door behind him. The air current caught her perfume, sweet and flowery.

"Okay, well, you've been here, this is the foyer. Unlike many bed and breakfasts that have been converted, my family built this home specifically to be a guesthouse in 1889. We have photos of the opening in the Tea Room. It must have been something. Anyway, the income paid the bills and allowed generations of Sutherlands to avoid being nine-to-fivers."

"I can understand that sentiment," Nate told her. "I would suffocate in an office building. So you were born into the business."

Hailey made a scoffing sound. "Not that I wanted to be. In fact, that's how I got engaged the first time."

Nate almost tripped. The *first* time?

"Fiancé Failure Number One was a dreamer. Not so much of a planner. Or a money saver. Anyway, my grandmother firmly believed the first thing any guest should see when they stepped inside The Sutherland was beauty."

It was an extreme effort to keep his eyes off of Hailey as she spoke. Now *that* was beauty. She spoke of her home with such passion he wanted to see what she saw, so he tore his gaze away from her smiling face. Waves of yellow sunlight poured from the double transoms, warm and welcoming. Just like Hailey.

"But now you're back, and clearly happy to be here," he said.

"The Sutherland needed me, and it's funny, but I found I needed it, too. I feel connected to my past now. See the staircase?" she asked.

Nate nodded. True to his prediction, he'd wanted to kick himself for not following his first instinct and explore where that staircase led with the woman beside him.

"At seventeen, it was my job to polish that sucker. I hated it, but now, when I see it gleam, I think about how my mother would let us slide down it when our father wasn't around."

He laughed at the image of this utterly feminine woman sliding down the banister like a tomboy.

"As you can see, we began by concentrating on the kitchen, Tea Room and terrace. The lobby is where we want to concentrate next. There are a dozen little Victorian touches we want to add to this room, like brocade or maybe some porcelain."

Nate had endured near freezing night swims and bunked under the stars in the desert and woken up with a mouthful of sand, but until a few days ago, he might have preferred a tent on the beach if presented with the idea of sleeping in a Victorian B&B. And if Hailey invited him up to her room…he might just endure Hell Week again for that. Hell, he was already getting hard.

"What else?" he asked in an effort to distract his mind from his body. And hers.

"Wireless Internet. All over." Hailey waved her hands dramatically. "You don't want to know," she said.

But he wanted to know. Know about her job, those cards, what she liked…anything she wanted to tell him.

The service door from the Tea Room to the kitchen opened and Amy walked in, looking rumpled and a cell phone to her ear.

"Jake, I don't want to talk about it. No, this is the way it has to be. I'm sorry. Okay, I'm at The Sutherland."

With a sad expression, she closed her phone, disconnecting the call. She looked up, jolted. Her hand flew to her neck. "Oh, you scared me. I didn't realize you two were in here."

"How's everything with Jake?" Hailey asked.

Amy's eyes filled with unshed tears. "He's still caught up that it's the card thing. I'm just going to go up to my room."

"What was that all about?" Jake couldn't help but ask after she'd gone.

"Those dumb Fate Delivery Cards." Hailey gave a theatrical shudder.

"Those cards seem to have something to answer for," he told her.

"Tell me about it," she said, her tone rueful. "Okay, let me put on my professional voice. 'Our hallmarks here at The Sutherland are our friendly and personal service, desserts and easy access to the beach. Whether you're on a business trip, looking for a romantic escape or a fun weekend away, we'll have the mojitos waiting.' Or at least that's how we're hoping it will be. As you can see, it's a work in progress."

"I can see that," he said and she laughed. "Are you ready to go?"

"Sure, what do you have planned?" she asked.

"It's a surprise."

"I hate surprises," Hailey said as she wrinkled her nose, and he fought the urge to kiss the tip of it. Then to move down to her lips and keep kissing.

"That's what I was counting on."

"As long as you brought the card I'll endure the surprise. Just be prepared to pay up on that one."

HAILEY HADN'T EXACTLY TOLD Nate the truth. She actually liked surprises, but only if she were the one giving the surprise. Now she was eaten up with curiosity by two things—what his card had instructed and what were they doing. Nate escorted her to a car that could only be described as a hotrod. Black, sleek and with its top down. "Bought it when I first joined the Navy and had that first flush of cash. Thought it was cool and the chicks would dig it. Didn't realize it would mainly sit in storage because I was always overseas. I've toyed with the idea of having it sent to Missouri for my brother to use."

"How'd a boy from Missouri wind up in the Navy?"

"It's funny, but a good portion of our ranks come from the land-locked states. Probably because we yearn to see the ocean."

He helped her inside the car and she was engulfed by the plush gray leather. The color matched his eyes, but she doubted he'd appreciate her pointing that out. He may think the car kind of silly now, but it suited him. Streamlined and amazing to look at. The car smelled like him, too—ocean breezes with a hint of wood and sea salt. She took a deep breath, and dragged in the scent of him.

"How long are you home?" she asked, as he joined her inside the car.

"Not much longer, I hope. Right now I'm instructing Land Nav for SEAL SQT."

She tried not to appear clueless.

"It's the last training the men have before becoming a SEAL," he explained.

Apparently she hadn't done such a good job in not seeming clueless.

"After BUD/S." A slow grin spread across his face, and his eyes twinkled. "None of this is ringing a bell, is it? I thought you grew up in San Diego."

"Yes, but my mom didn't let me hang around sailors."

"Smart mom," he said, laughter in his voice.

Tell me about it. With his tight military-trained body, easy good looks and on the lookout for a fun time, he was like her kryptonite. "Sorry I'm so unfamiliar."

"Actually, I kind of like it."

After they fastened their seatbelts, Nate fired the powerful engine and they were off. He easily navigated away from Coronado toward old San Diego. She breathed deep as they crossed the Coronado Bridge linking the two areas. Soon she spotted the Victorian era buildings that could only be the historic Gaslamp Quarter. The city and its residents had done an amazing job restoring this area, and now it was a major attraction, from the Horton Grand Theater to antiques shops.

She turned toward him. "I've been wanting to visit Gaslamp since I came home, just never had the time."

"Thought seeing all this restoration would be inspiring."

"Me, too." And they shared one of those endless kinds of stares girls dreamed about as longing-for-a-boyfriend teenagers. The kind of gaze that never grew awkward, but instead only made them more aware of each other as a man and as a woman. And she was very much aware of him as a man. Her skin heated.

Nate had planned this just for her. He'd actually thought about it and attempted to come up with something for them to do that she would like.

She could be in some trouble with this one.

After Nate parked and put up the top, they strolled though Gaslamp. "I'll have to bring you back here at night. The Gaslamp Quarter sign is all lit up."

A warm tremble settled in her stomach hearing him suggest future times together.

More kryptonite.

They strolled through several unique stores of the Quarter and then Nate led her to an antique shop. She was intrigued by so many of the wares and displays that the only thing that had a hope of interrupting her was the growl of her stomach. Which it did. Loudly.

"One quick stop and then we can eat," he promised.

The crowds outside on the sidewalk were heavier now than when they first hit Gaslamp, and it seemed the most natural thing in the world for her to accept Nate's hand. The man was commanding in a crowd, people seemed to naturally get out of his way. The two of them walked together until they stood outside one of the oldest hotels of the area.

Irritation tensed her stomach, chasing away her earlier warmer feelings. Just what did he think was going to happen here? At a hotel? She followed him to the ornately carved front desk. The reception area was a classic example of Victorian-era American furnishings, with its dark woods and interiors. The Sutherland's front desk was not nearly as dramatic as the one here, but it was clear they were cousins. Although hers were the poorer relations.

"There should be a basket for Peterson."

That caught her attention. So he wasn't planning on checking in for a little first date horizontal time. That flash of irritation she'd felt, she now directed at herself. She shouldn't be so quick to judge on the basis of past bad boyfriends.

The woman behind the desk smiled and picked up the phone. "Let me just ring dining."

This was getting stranger. Nate reached for his wallet, and she discreetly walked away from the transaction. That move was squarely from her father's Rules of Dating 101. You never paid attention to how much or how little a man spent on a date. Instead she busied herself admiring the handpainted wallpaper with its stylized flowers and leaves the color of jasper—straight from the Victorian era. The fabric of the chairs in the lobby matched the wallpaper. What a good idea.

After a moment, a woman bustled up from the dining room carrying a large wicker hamper that looked a lot like a—

"Here's your picnic basket." She flashed a friendly smile toward Hailey. "Hope you enjoy your day."

"A picnic basket?" she asked as they were once more outside, her hand back in his.

"Unlike you, I'm not much of a cook."

He'd brought the romantic big gun, and Hailey realized she wasn't as immune as she'd suggested to Nate their last time together. Her heart, or stomach or something inside her seemed to soften. Hailey took a deep breath.

Then they were back in his car and this time they traveled up the San Diego freeway until she made out a familiar sign. "You're not taking me to Sea World?" she teased.

"I'm saving that for another day," he said with a wink. "We're going to Mission Bay Park."

The Mission Bay area had been a favorite of hers growing up. Acres and acres of nothing but green grass, palm trees and sandy beaches. The perfect place for a picnic. She had to reassess her beliefs about military men. Nate had whipped up something very romantic. For her. The predictable heartmelting reaction followed. This was even worse than softening. She really needed to avoid romance.

They took a winding path until they reached a shady spot. Nate spread out the traditional red and white-checkered cloth and they both sunk to the comfortable ground, softened by grass and blanket.

The basket contained delicious chicken salad, fresh fruit, croissants and wine, and since it was food she didn't have to prepare, cook or clean up afterward, Hailey was thrilled. "I have to hand it to you, Nate, this has been a really fun time."

"I'm glad. The hotel even tucked a kite inside the basket," he said.

Just to make sure every romantic date cliché had been covered. Unfortunately, it was working.

He stood, towering above her. Nate offered her his hand again, and although she'd held it before, she could dismiss that as an act of crowd protection. This time it would be more personal. Intimate. And why was she overanalyzing something like simply holding hands?

Nate had a man's hand. Big and callused and that easily engulfed hers. With little effort he tugged her to her feet. She grew increasingly aware of every inch of his body as he pulled her up. The wetsuit had only hinted at the strength of his legs, the utter flatness of his stomach and solidness of his chest. Without her heels, the top of her head was somewhere in the vicinity of his nose, and when she reached her full height she was staring at the jut of his chin. A chin with just a hint of a dimple.

It was one of the sexiest things she'd ever seen. She lifted her hand to trace it, then pulled away swiftly. Had she lost her mind? Hailey's eyes settled on the line of his mouth, his bottom lip surprisingly curved. Finally she met his gaze. And sucked in a breath.

He'd been waiting for her to meet his gaze. Where once she only saw the color of cool gray steel, his eyes had now darkened to a smoky slate. He wanted her. Hailey's heart began to pound. Her lips parted and she leaned into him. She wanted to kiss him so bad.

"This part of the park is perfect for kite flying. No power lines. No tall trees. You ready?"

She was ready for something, she just wasn't sure what.

That was a look of desire he flashed her, right? Hailey had chosen not to date for a while, but surely she wouldn't miss the mark that much? She'd certainly flashed him all the signs that she was ready for a little lip action.

"I can't remember the last time I flew a kite," she told him with a smile. Her voice tight.

He dropped her hands, then reached for the kite. It wasn't anything fancy—a few wooden poles, thin cotton material, but the tail…now that was cool. All the different, brightly colored fabrics tied to the string invited her enthusiasm.

"You want to toss up the kite or hold the string?" he asked.

"String."

He flashed her a boyish grin, handing her the string while holding the kite with excitement. Obviously she'd chosen correctly. "Okay, give it a little slack."

"Now what?" she asked when standing a few yards away.

"We wait for the wind."

A quick gust from off the ocean zoomed in, and Nate tossed the kite up. The air caught it at the right angle and the material poofed and lifted. She gave it more string, instinct or some muscle memory from child-hood activated, and soon she had their yellow kite flying high in the air.

He returned to her side. His eyes were trained to the sky. "Pretty good teamwork," he said.

They stood together, side by side, watching as the kite went higher and higher. "Want to run with it?" she asked, feeling light and carefree and wanting the wind on her face and in her hair.

"Absolutely. We should lower it some. I'll help," he offered. Nate looped his arms over her shoulders and then his hands surrounded hers. Once again she was struck by just how big he was. How much larger he was than she. Like a mismatch. But with his tanned arms circling hers she had a great view of the hardened muscles of his biceps. Staring at the kite and running with it wasn't the same kind of temptation it was a moment ago. Now she battled leaning fully against him, closing her eyes and breathing him in.

"You know, I think there are easier ways to rein in the kite," she said over her shoulder.

He nodded. "Probably." But he didn't move.

She laughed and together they towed the kite lower until it bounced and waved only a few feet above their heads. Then he found her hand, and the two of them ran down the sandy beach, the water tickling their toes. They dodged children splashing in the foam and seashells and Hailey laughed, really laughed. Had she ever laughed this way with a man?

To her surprise the wind died, and their kite fell to the ground. "Oh, that's too bad," she said, her tone full of regret.

"Not really." And for her second surprise Nate brought her chin up and his lips came down on hers. Hailey didn't know how long they kissed under the sun with the waves lapping at her feet, but it was the most amazing kiss of her life. *This* was what it felt like to have Nate fully involved with a kiss from the beginning. That Fate Card sure knew how to deliver.

His lips moved along hers with a gentle confidence. She rose on her tiptoes and draped her arms around his shoulders. Nate's hands found her hips, and he nestled her closer into his body as his tongue found hers. He tasted like wine and a sunny day and she couldn't get enough of it.

The breeze picked up again, and she heard the kite kick and crash against the sand. Nate's hands slowly drifted up her waist and over her arms to cup her face. With a reluctance she wasn't quite ready to acknowledge, she allowed Nate to draw her away. He rested his forehead to hers and she felt him take a deep breath.

Hailey smiled, knowing the kiss had affected him as much as it had wrecked havoc with her.

"After BUD/S, I never thought I'd *want* to run on the beach again."

Warmth spread through her chest at his rueful words. She liked knowing she could change his mind.

"Of course then I'd just swam, jogged and then told to roll in the sand. I came out looking like a sugar cookie."

Now that held some strange appeal. Nate had conjured up in her mind two delicious images, cookies, and a wet, buff man in a swimsuit.

"You ready to finish off that wine?" he asked.

No, but it would have to do. She nodded, and after winding the remaining kite string up tight, they returned to the blanket.

They lay on the checkered material, facing one another. The breeze and warm sunny day lulled her, tempted her to lower her guard where Nate was concerned. Thoughts like, "what could it hurt to see him a few times?" and "he'll be gone soon, no harm, no foul, right?" kept popping into her head. And of course everything about him from his consideration to his tight butt lured her further into thinking about taking everything he offered and demanding more.

Soon the sex thoughts emerged. She'd had the emo artist guy, the business-suited manipulator and finally Mr. Hot who was as into himself as she was into him. But she'd never been intimate with the hard body, capable type. Broad shoulders, strong arms...she had more than one thing to be thankful to the U.S. military for. What would he be like in bed? Adjectives like maneuverable and robust popped into her head, and she fought a giggle.

Then words like powerful, strong and big pushed those other words aside. The man jumped out of planes, he dived under water with explosives strapped to his body with only his ability and equipment to trust. The man possessed that quiet intensity that both excited and unnerved her. What would it be like to have all that focused directly on her? As they made love? Hailey shivered. The idea was both delicious and intimidating. Actually, very intimidating.

"Grape?" he asked.

It was clear he planned to feed her. It was right up there on the romantic scale, and must have been his one-thousandth sexy move of the day. Why had she ever mentioned she didn't believe in romance? Hailey drained her wineglass. Now was the time to remind him of her no relationship stipulation because this felt very much like a relationship oriented moment. With a sigh she said, "I just want to make sure you know…I don't date."

He nodded, looking completely unconcerned.

"At all," she added for emphasis.

"I remember," he told her, his eyes growing curious. "How come?"

"I pick bad men."

His lips twisted, and he gave her a kind of lopsided grin. "It's a good thing you didn't pick me then. Your Fate Delivery Card did, remember?"

Exactly how much sexiness and allure was a woman supposed to take? Man, if ever the "life wasn't fair" assertion had come into play. This was it. When she didn't want a man, a funny hot one charged onto the scene. She had to put an end to this now, or she'd be back down that same road. She was supposed to be taking time off. Regrouping, and yes it was a cliché, but finding herself.

"Enough with the charm," she said with a good-natured, but very firm, grin.

"I balk at the word charm."

She knew his shmooze was all in an effort to prove her wrong. "Okay, attitude then. It's cute, but I've done the cute fiancé thing. In fact, I've had three."

"Three?" he asked, his voiced raised since the first time she'd met him.

Now he sounded a little concerned. He should be concerned. She'd tried to warn him.

"I thought I only had to contend with one former fiancé, but three?"

So, he'd put some thought into her brief mention of her former lover. It made her happy despite the fact that there would be no place for them to go with what they were doing.

"I'm taking time off from men."

"Strange, it seemed like I was getting a very different signal from you when you were in my arms, kissing me."

"I wasn't kissing you, you were kissing me."

"You were kissing my face off."

She propped her hands on her hips. "I was not. It was fun, I grant you that, but it was part of the mood—the kite, the beach, the running. It was the scenario, and I doubt the mood will strike again."

As soon as the words flew out of her mouth, she knew she'd said the wrong thing. Nate was the kind of guy who *enjoyed* a challenge. Hell, he probably lived for the adrenaline rush.

"Listen, if you want to try it again just to prove it didn't mean anything, you're welcome to." He flexed the muscles across his chest as if he was bracing himself.

She laughed, but quickly cleared her expression. "I think I've seen that ploy in a movie or something. Look, we're not going to act out any cutesy scene of you daring me to kiss you and if I don't respond then you'll go away."

"Kiss you again? I hadn't even thought of that."

"Liar. I'm just going to lay it all on the line here." Enough with the playful banter. It was time to get serious. "You are very good-looking, sexy even."

"Why am I not feeling flattered?"

Hailey smiled. "Ordinarily I'd be going for you in a snap, and therefore," Hailey held up her hands and said, "I'm not."

The humor faded from his eyes. "That makes zero sense."

"Believe me, you don't want to know how many mistakes I've made with men. Sure I could get involved with you, I mean, what girl wouldn't want to at least try to make something work with you? Normally, I'd be there in a shot and it would be great…for awhile. But then what would happen? My very prominent self-destructive DNA asserts itself."

Nate glanced around the park. Searching for an escape route perhaps? "Usually I follow one of two routes. Option one is me finding fault with every little thing you do. Men love a nagging woman, believe me."

"What if there's nothing to find fault with?"

Ah, more of that challenging spirit. She liked it.

"Well then, I go into my test mode. That's were I see how much of my nonsense you'd take. Either way, the sex gets really awkward, and eventually you'll have had enough. Then starts the dividing of our stuff, and…right now you should be thanking your lucky stars that I'm preemptively ending our relationship before it even starts."

"Huh, and here I was thinking maybe dinner. Did you say something about sex in all that?" he asked. He stroked down her forearm with the back of his hand. The warmth of his caress made her jolt.

Funny, sexy and charming…her doom. *Get away from him now.*

"Do I make you nervous, Hailey?" By the stunned expression on his face, he seemed surprised by his re-alization.

Yes. "No, uh, no. Of course not. Why do you ask?" She glanced downward, and began to play with the edge of the blanket.

His hands stilled hers, and she looked up. "You seem jumpy around me. Although you're awfully girly, you don't seem high-strung, so I'm guessing it's me," he said his tone light, but his expression serious.

And he got it in one. He made her nervous and jumpy and agitated in ways no man ever had. But she would not be intimidated by her primal reaction to the man. No, she'd give as good as she got. "Girly?" she questioned.

Hailey imagined some lean, athletic type woman who would look great with her hair in a ponytail, no make-up and jogging beside this very physical man. In school she'd always admired the girls on the soccer field running and laughing. Hailey didn't even have the coordination to do step aerobics.

"I take it you don't normally go for the girly types."

He shook his head, his smile turning rueful. "No one ever baked me cookies," he said, his voice low and raspy.

His tone told her he wanted to taste her cookies like he wanted to taste her.

"And those dresses you wear with the frilly little straps…"

Nate's voice trailed, and she imagined his lean fingers sliding those straps down her shoulders.

"Or worn an apron," he said, leaning closer. "I just want to reach for the strap and tug."

She swallowed, thinking of him taking off her apron…and more.

"And those ridiculous heels are sexy as hell," he whispered against her lips. Then his mouth settled on hers, warm and inviting and for way, way too short of a time.

After she caught her breath, she smiled up into his eyes. "I'm good with girly."

His eyes darkened, and his gaze made a pass to her lips, down to her breasts, then back up to meet her eyes. "I'm more than good with it."

7

SOMEHOW, SOMEWAY, Hailey found herself on the date that would never end. A date she didn't *want* to end. Nate seemed just as reluctant to leave because now he sat on the terrace of the Sutherland drinking a beer. She hadn't been able to convince him to sample the Mojito.

Alone with nothing but the breeze and the peaceful lap of the ocean, Hailey became utterly aware that she was alone in the dark with Nate. A man she couldn't wait to get her hands on. She'd never diss romance again because right now the butterflies were making an appearance in her stomach. Not even the moon was out to shed light between them, and her senses grew hyper-alert of every subtle shift of his body.

He stood, and Hailey sucked in a breath, instantly feeling foolish.

"Do I make you nervous, Hailey?" he asked, his voice like a caress to her already agitated senses.

"You…you asked me that once already."

"And then I got distracted, but I'm not distracted now. Now I'm focused on you."

That's what she was afraid of. To have all that single-minded SEAL determination and intensity focused squarely on her…heady.

With one quick, silent motion, he was beside her. His big body warm and oh, so tempting. "How'd you do that? I can't see a thing out here in the dark." Besides being night, the awning partially covering the terrace shrouded them in shadows.

"Most of my missions are after the sun sets. SEALs do their best work in the dark."

That's what she was afraid of.

He trailed a finger down her cheek, making her shiver. "So what's the problem?" he asked.

How like Nate to want to tackle a problem head on. Based on the several personality quizzes she'd taken over the years, she knew she preferred to be an avoider in bad situations.

Whoa, and there was another problem. She'd only known the man a few days, and already she was recognizing his personality traits. Hailey swallowed. She was on a mission to change, might as well take a cue from the man she found so intriguing. "You're a little…a little big."

Hailey could almost feel him smile. Yeah, yeah yeah, she knew where his thinking was headed because her mind had also gone *there,* too.

He gently cupped her face, kissed the tip of her nose. "I could never hurt you, Hailey."

She nodded. "I know."

"No, I mean, Hailey, I would never hurt you. Never *allow* anything to hurt you."

Her throat tightened. Nate's words were the sexiest, most amazing thing a man had ever said to her. And she knew, deep down, he meant it.

"I'll prove it," he offered.

He must have taken her silence for doubt. She

almost rushed to reassure him, but a very intriguing thought popped into her head. "How would you prove it, Nate?" she asked.

"You be in control. You tell me how to touch your body. Where to kiss. When to move."

Every nerve ending, every muscle, every sense she had popped into action. If she'd thought having all his intensity focused on her was heady, his offer now made her lightheaded. Her nipples tightened. Warmth pooled between her legs. "I just tell you what to do?"

"If anything you suggest shocks me, I'll let you know," he said, his voice teasing and yet filled with so much desire for her that Hailey's nerves began to subside.

What did she want him to do to her? For her? In the past, she'd concentrated on how to make the men in her life happy, but here was one wanting to see to her needs. "Kiss my face," she encouraged. "Gentle, but not on my lips."

Nate drew her head toward his mouth, and ran his lips lightly along the line of her jaw, kissed her chin, then the tip of her nose. Finally, he tenderly kissed her closed eyes. Heaven.

"Trace my lips with your tongue."

His strong arms circled her shoulders, bringing her nearer. Slowly, achingly slow, his tongue followed the line of her bottom lip, then the top. She wanted him to sink his tongue into her mouth, sensed he wanted to deepen the caress as well, but didn't. True to his word, he was waiting for the invitation.

"Kiss me," she urged. With a groan, his tongue slid past her lips and teeth to tangle with her tongue. How quickly she had become accustomed to his taste.

Her nipples tightened further. Her breasts ached for his touch.

"Caress my breasts."

Nate's hands flowed down her body until they rested at her hips. His fingers slipped under the material of her shirt, and she sucked in a breath at the exquisite feel of his warm fingers against the bare skin of her stomach. If this is what he could do with just a touch to her waist, imagine what the man could do when he had free rein of her body.

His hands slowly drifted up her sides, past her ribcage and finally cupped her breasts. "You fill my hands perfectly," he whispered against her lips.

Hailey had not always been a fan of her small breasts. Had even thought of augmenting them at one time, but right now she couldn't be happier with their size. "Take my bra off and really feel them," she said, surprised by the impatience she heard in her voice.

His fingers made a lazy trail to her back where he found the clasp. With a quick motion, he freed her breasts, cupping them once more.

"Does this seat lay back?" he asked.

"Yes."

Hailey felt cold as his hands left her body, but the idea of stretching out on the lounger with Nate beside her was just too appealing.

"Take my shirt off," she said. Nate's fingers tugged the material up and over her head, tossing it to the side.

Hailey slipped her bra off and reclined against the cushion.

"I wish I could see you," he said, his voice raw and filled with wanting.

"I thought you said SEALs worked best in the dark."

"After lots of practice. I'm going to need a lot of time with your body," he responded.

There were the shivers again. "Then have at it," she invited.

"No, you have to tell me what to do. Remember?"

If those weren't the sexiest words ever spoken by a man, she didn't know what would qualify. She swallowed, readying herself to tell this man in detail what she wanted him to do to her body.

"I want you to gently touch my breasts with the palms of your hands. Slowly. In circles."

The lounger dipped as he leaned toward her, and then she felt the heat of his hands, smoothing over her nipples.

"Lighter," she instructed, and sucked in a breath as the pressure of his stroking eased to just a hint of a touch.

"Mmm, I like that." And she wanted more. "Now I want you to lick my nipples then blow."

Nate followed her instructions as if he was born to do it; the sensations exquisite. "My nipples are so tight."

"I know, I want to suck them."

Moist heat flooded between her legs. "Well, you can't," she teased, feeling powerful and in control—exactly the way Nate wanted her to feel. "I want you to tease my nipples, gently with your teeth."

With a swirl of his tongue, he did just that. First one nipple, then the other. Her toes curled into the cushion, he was making her feel so good. Hailey felt the solid length of his erection against her thigh. Clearly, the man was big all over.

It took a moment for her to find her voice. "Now I want you to trace my entire body with your hands, making your circles smaller and smaller until you reach my…"

"Your what?" he asked against her ear. His warm breath tickled her neck and sent shivers through her body.

He was going to make her say it. "My clit."

"You have on too many clothes," he stated.

"Then take them off."

"As you command." She knew Nate was smiling in the dark because she was, too. His fingers found the waistband of her pants, and pulled them slowly down, down her legs.

Hailey sat up on her elbows. "But wait, you left my panties."

"Do you want me to take them off?" he asked, but his promising tone made her think she might want Nate to take her clothes off in stages.

She shook her head and lowered herself back against the soft cushion of the lounger. "No. Leave them."

Nate started with his circles, his hands not touching anyplace remotely sexual as he stroked her in a wide arc. Her heels dug deeper and deeper into the lounger as his circles tightened. He reached the top swell of her breasts, down her arms and across her thighs.

Now his hands were fully across her nipples making them tingle, then his brief touch moved lower to torment her thighs, getting closer and closer to the spot she knew he'd make her feel best.

Two more circles around her body and his hand settled between her legs. With a slow, tortuous glide his hand slid between her thighs to stop at the silk of her panties.

Frustration bubbled up inside her. "Take them off."

"How? With my hands or with my teeth?"

Her legs began to shake. "Teeth," she urged.

Hailey felt his lips at the place where skin met silk.

He gently kissed her hip, traced the edge of lace with his tongue, then he nipped at the material, drawing it into his mouth. She squeezed her eyes tight as the amazing sensations of those panties sliding down her body, dragged only by Nate's teeth.

He finally had her naked. His fingers started to slowly trace her again. This time he didn't stop anywhere. No, now his fingers slid up between her thighs. And up until his fingers tickled the curls. Then he stopped.

The waiting was agony. Why wasn't he doing anything? Then she realized he was waiting for her next instruction.

"Stroke me," she said, her voice strained.

And Nate slipped a finger inside her, and tenderly began to move. "Touch me more," she commanded, never feeling so raw. Nate slipped another finger inside and his thumb finally, *finally* touched her clit. A moan tore from her body and she began to writhe. Something was missing. She was astounded by her overwhelming desire to have him *fill* her. She'd never felt that way.

"Now, Nate. I need you now."

"I don't have a condom," he told her.

She almost groaned. "What? Why?" she asked.

"I was supposed to be romancing you tonight. If I'd brought a condom I'd be thinking about sex," he said with a laugh.

How like him to psych himself up that way.

"But don't worry, I can still take care of you," he promised, his voice sensual, his words sincere.

Hailey was wet now. Nate's lips touched hers at the

same time his thumb settled on her clit. His fingers began to slide in and out of her. She raised her hips toward his hand, not able to get enough of him.

"This is how I'll make love to you," he said against her mouth. "Gentle until you want it hard."

"I want it hard *now*." She was breathless. Sweat broke out along her forehead.

And Nate complied with her wish, his fingers all over, all in her until that sweet tension inside broke and she erupted. Her moan filled the air as she came.

After a few minutes, when her breathing returned to normal, Nate tenderly kissed her face. The tip of her nose. Her eyes. Just like her first instructions.

"Do I still make you nervous?" he asked.

Even more so. A man who could make her respond to him like she had with just one hand was a man to be concerned about.

But her worries about his bigness, about his overwhelming power had subsided. "Yes," she replied, nodding.

He sat up, flexing the muscles of his shoulder. The lounger was oversized, but it wasn't built for two, and with Nate's large frame, that had to have been a tight squeeze. "I better go," he said.

"Oh, but what about, uh, you." Nate had to be in a bad way.

He felt around at his feet until he found her clothes. "We'll take care of me next time."

Next time. His words made her skin tingle. Hailey couldn't wait until they took care of him.

He helped her with her clothes, and then walked her to the terrace door. The parking lot was as easily assessable from the terrace as it was the front door. "Nate, make sure you bring a condom."

A slow smile tugged at his lips. "I'll bring more than one. Now lock the door."

With a twist of her wrist, she made sure The Sutherland was secure for the night. Nate checked the lock from the outside then turned. She watched his retreating back until she couldn't see him anymore.

Hailey knew she wore a goofy grin, but she couldn't help it. The man made her feel amazing, but there was something else. That checking the door move made her heart skip a beat. What had her first instinct been about the man? That he was trouble?

Instincts usually seemed to be right.

"Oh, Hailey, there you are."

Hailey spun around to spot Amy at the entrance of the Tea Room and her hand went immediately to her hair. Did she look normal, or did she look like a woman who'd just—

"Do you have a few moments? I wanted to talk to you about Jake."

Whew, okay, maybe she didn't look too rumpled. Or sated. Hailey pulled out one of the Queen Anne chairs from the closest table and invited Amy to take a seat. "How are things with Jake?"

Amy's face crumpled, yet she managed to appear a bit defiant. "He's still pretty angry with me."

"Well, I can kind of see his point."

Amy gasped.

Okay, Hailey obviously needed a more tactful approach here. She schooled her features into what she hoped was an understanding expression, and faced her confused and upset guest and friend. "I mean, you won't even see him, Amy. That kind of sounds like you're following the instructions of the card rather than trying to discover the source of your problems together as a couple."

"I keep telling myself if it's meant to be then it's meant to be."

A trickle of unease slid down Hailey's back. What Amy had just said wasn't something she hadn't thought of herself half a dozen times, but now…now it seemed a little like leaving things in fate's hands. And she was pretty irritated with fate right now. First by delivering a man she couldn't stop thinking about, but knew she should stay away from, and now a friend turned guest whose life was in shambles because of what happened at The Sutherland. Not exactly a great restart for their B&B.

That reminded her. They were going to burn Amy's card and never had. Tonight would be a great time to do it. In fact, they could burn the whole deck right here at the—

"Do you ever have to fake it?" Amy asked.

Well, there'd certainly been no pretending with Nate. Hailey glanced toward the door, wanting to escape. Where was her sister when she needed her?

"Would you like me to brew some chamomile?"

Amy shook her head. "No, if I don't do this now, have a real conversation about sex, I might be miserable for the rest of my life." Amy grew flustered. "Jake's the only man I've been with, and I've never been particularly adventurous. Well, sometimes he would like me to be…"

Hailey reached for her hand and gave her a reassuring squeeze. Wow, what kind of freaky stuff was this man into to make Amy so upset? "It's okay, you can tell me anything. Go on."

"Sometimes he would like me to be on top," Amy said on a rush of exhaled breath.

Hailey turned skeptical. "Are you…kidding with me?"

"No, no. There's more. He once told me he'd like for me to initiate sex once in a while, can you believe it?"

Hailey chewed on her bottom lip.

"I know there are women, friends of ours who have no problem being so wild, but I've tried and I just can't do it."

Hailey let out a relieved sigh. "For a minute there, I was afraid you were going to tell me he was into something really weir—okay, I'm not doing such a good job here. Amy, it seems like you were born before the sexual revolution. What you've said doesn't even describe *my* mom. I know your grandparents raised you, but surely…"

"My grandmother told me sex—" Amy smiled, obviously proud she was able to say the word without stumbling "—was something you did to make your husband happy, and that was basically my entire education. When she had to buy me my first B, I thought I was going to die of embarrassment."

"Are you still calling it that?"

Amy nodded.

"I'm almost feeling sorry for Jake," muttered Hailey.

Amy looked hurt.

"I keep saying the wrong thing, don't I? I'm so sorry." Where was her sister?

Surprisingly, Amy chuckled. "Oh. My. God. What kind of grown woman can't say the word bra?"

The two of them laughed together, but Hailey quickly sobered. "Just so I'm clear, you've never had an orgasm?"

"I don't think so."

"Believe me, there's no 'think' about it if you've had one." Hailey's body warmed at the memory of the orgasm Nate had given her a little while ago. "I'll put that down as a no. You've never done anything other than the, uh, missionary position?"

Amy shook her head quickly, her cheeks glowing pink.

Hailey shook her head again. "I can't believe Jake even got you into the bedroom."

"To tell you the truth, I can't believe it either. I was liking it up to a point, all the kissing and the holding, but then I felt so dirty."

Hailey made a disgusted noise. "I can't believe you were ever taught to feel that way. Sex, making love, it's a wonderful thing. It can draw a couple together and be beautiful, or it can be playful and fun, and sometimes you could maybe make it dirty," Hailey said, and winked, "if you wanted to. But sex can also divide two people, and that sounds like what's going on between you and Jake."

"Like a wedge," Amy agreed.

"I'm guessing that you've never discussed this with your fiancé? Or anyone?"

"Oh, God no. I turn on the water faucet when I go to the bathroom, I certainly couldn't talk to him about *this*." She shook her head. "Even when I moved into the dorms at school, some of the girls made fun of me, so I kept my mouth shut."

Hailey sucked in her lip, feeling guilty all over again. "Have I apologized about laughing earlier?"

Flashing her an easy grin, Amy said, "Tori just thinks I'm shy. No one, but you, knows it all."

"I'm going to say it again. The person you need to be talking to is Jake."

"No I couldn't."

"You're going to have to do something. Believe me when I tell you this, Jake appears to be a hell of a guy, especially considering the water bill he must be facing. But sex is important in a relationship. You need to fix this now. Listen, I have an idea. I'm going to run up to my room and grab something for you. Be right back."

"Okay," Amy said, and Hailey bound from the room.

Hailey returned, holding a small red and yellow book. *Freeing Your Sexual Self.* Amy swallowed after reading the title.

Hailey gave Amy's shoulder a reassuring pat. "Don't let the title intimidate you. Also, maybe you're thinking about your Fate Delivery Card in the wrong way."

"How could I look at it any other way? Picking *that* card…it was just so strange. There's fate, and there's co-incidence and then there's plain cosmic weirdness. Surely there was a reason, two weeks before I'm supposed to get married, that I pull that card from the deck. Right? How many signs am I supposed to ignore?"

Hailey's head tilted. "Or those 'signs' just mani-fested in the form of silly little cards that mean nothing and you're in the middle of a sex wedge and some very understandable prewedding jitters and panicked."

Amy glanced down at the engagement ring twin-kling on her finger. "The card only made it clear to me that things have been off for a while."

Hailey held up her hands in surrender. "I've had

three failed engagements, maybe some of my bad luck is rubbing off on you."

Amy quickly looked up at her new friend. "Of course not, that's just silly."

"As silly as banking your future on some mass produced boxed card set? Anyway, this is what I meant about the card. Maybe you're not supposed to set him free as in letting him go. Maybe you're supposed to set something in your relationship free, as in exploring. Now, get to reading." Hailey stood. "I'll leave you to it."

8

"THOSE CHOCOLATE and strawberry waffles are to die for. The guests are asking for more," Hailey informed her sister, as she placed the serving tray on the tiled countertop. Nate liked good food. Would he feel like breakfast in bed?

"How's our latest guest doing?" Rachel asked. The line forming between her eyebrows told Hailey how worried her sister was.

"Relax, I set a few things in motion last night. I'm sure the self-help book I gave her really got her mind to thinking."

Rachel groaned. "Not another one." Her sister took a very deep breath. "It's okay. Not going to worry about it. What was it mom always said? Don't get involved with the lives of guests?"

"Amy is not a guest, she's Amy. And if that's a rule, we can add it to the long list of other ones I've broken. We stayed up pretty late last night talking."

"Get any closer to her real reason for being so upset?"

"Yes, and believe me, you don't want to hear it."

"Good, I don't. Did you see that? *That* is how you take sound advice."

Hailey laughed. She felt kind of sorry for Amy—not

having a sister to laugh with, talk about sex with, get advice from.

"By the way, how did everything go last night? I had the ice cream all ready," Rachel said.

Hailey heard the disappointment in her sister's voice and immediately felt guilty. Eating ice cream in the kitchen after a date had become a tradition when their mom was still alive. The three of them would joke, confide, eat and talk about their date until her dad would tease them that girl power hour was over.

"Rachel, I'm sorry. I guess I've been going on dates and dissecting them all on my own for so long, I completely forgot." Not that she hadn't already dissected every moment, every touch and every kiss she'd shared with Nate.

"Waffle batter is not as fun as hot fudge and sprinkles, but you're going to spill it all right now. Did you get lips?"

She shivered at the memory. "As in non-card-coerced-mouth-on-mouth action?"

"Stop stalling. I'm not afraid to splash you with melted butter."

"Okay, yes, I got lips." And so much more. "If I were the kind of girl that appreciated romance and romantic gestures, I'd say he scored himself a winner. A picnic on the beach." And she wanted even more than what she got although she knew she shouldn't. She was man transitioning here.

Rachel dropped the sponge in the murky water. "Wait, what? You did something outside? On purpose? And you liked it? With the bugs, and the probability of sweating and the potential to mess your hair?"

"I'm not that bad."

"Yeah, I'm actually giving you a little credit. Hailey, you're my sister and I love you, but you're the girliest girl I know. Pink is your favorite color and there hasn't been a pair of cute strappy sandals you could say no to. I didn't even know you owned a pair of tennis shoes until I saw you walk out of here in them with Nate."

"I'd just bought them," Hailey confessed. Then busied her hands arranging the glasses on the top rack of the commercial dishwasher.

Rachel shook her head. "Wow, I get more and more impressed by this SEAL the more I hear about him. He got you into something totally ungirly."

He could probably get her out of something just as easily.

"So, when are you going out again?"

Hailey stopped loading the dishwasher. "He didn't exactly ask me for another date." He'd just referred to *next time*.

The teasing smile faded from her sister's face. "Hmm, that's odd. He seemed pretty into you."

"I told him I didn't do relationships." She almost wished she'd kept her mouth closed.

Her sister clucked her tongue. "I knew you wouldn't take my advice. Feel free to ignore the little sister. He didn't seem the type to be discouraged that easily."

No, Nate was clearly one of those over-achiever types. And where were all these conflicted feelings coming from? She didn't want to date right now. Did she? She'd had to remind herself of that several times last night when he reached for her hand as they strolled on the sidewalk. She clearly recapped her resolution as they raced down the beach with the kite. Okay, she forgot during the kissing part, but that was a minor slip off course. She was back, repeating the no-dating mantra, when they were lying on the blanket together, enjoying the wine.

But then all hell broke loose out there on the terrace.

"You're smiling," Rachel said.

"What?" she asked. Playing it dumb was the best course of action here.

"You don't look like he took your words at face value. Like maybe something a little more than lips happened last night."

"I don't know what you're talking about," she insisted as she closed the door to the dishwasher. A little too forcefully.

"Listen, if you can't be honest with yourself, at least be honest with me. You like him."

Hailey pressed the button to get the machine started, then propped her hip against the counter. "Now is not the best time for me to be seeing him. To be seeing anyone."

"So why did you agree?"

Because when he was sitting here in this kitchen it seemed like a really good idea. Nate was funny, and charming and so, *so* hot.

"You're going to hate it when I tell you. He took a Fate Delivery Card, and…" Hailey's words trailed away on a gasp. "All the time he never told me what it said on his card," Hailey blurted, feeling really naive.

That kiss he'd given her had really messed with her priorities.

"Maybe that was his plan," Rachel said.

And it was a pretty good one. Her curiosity ramped even higher now, and it wasn't only about the card.

She was intrigued about the man, his motives and how he'd make love.

"Well, anyway. Enough about Nate. I have some good news, too. My friend at the Tourism Bureau came through. We have at least twelve guests for coffee and cake. Operation Spot a SEAL two point oh is on."

TONIGHT'S TRAINING EXERCISES would take them late until the evening. They'd fast rope from the helo at sunset, swim for two hours, then ascend to the helicopter in the dark. SEALs conducted the majority of their operations at night to avoid detection. These men would not only have to get used to the dark, but qualify to where they operated in the shadows just as easily as in the daylight. For Nate it was his everyday job, but the training had to reflect the realities of life as a SEAL. The new moon would give them no help.

No one spoke, each man concentrating on the job. They were getting closer to completing SQT, closer to earning their Trident, which finally made them a SEAL. Still, even at this level, some would fall short.

In a few minutes, The Sutherland would come into view. Nate couldn't imagine the B&B without thinking of the action that took place outside between him and Hailey. Damn, that woman was hot. He could still hear those quick breaths she took. Or that sexy slow moan she made as she turned to fire in his arms. Adrenaline rushed through him, searing his focus. He was always like this before a jump, but this time he was more tense because he wanted to see if Hailey had kept her word about no more women on the shoreline.

Truthfully, he expected his men to operate as trained

regardless if a hundred flashing women waited for them at the beach. Good experience for his men to work through the distraction. His hand fisted around his harness. Except that it would mean something—something *to him,* if the ladies weren't there all scantily clad and cheering. Hailey would have placed his request above her own financial gain. Long before she'd told him, it was obvious that she needed the money and he knew what it would cost her not to have the extra cash from those women.

He held his breath and glanced down at the beach, but the helo was still too far away for him to get a clear picture. Nate noticed some of the men were also straining to see if their cheerleaders were on the beach. Didn't matter. The rush provided by the thought of those women might give the men an edge.

He shifted in his seat, his gaze never settling for very long. What waited or didn't wait on the beach would answer a lot of questions. Like whether he should go with his gut, instead of his head, and pursue Hailey.

The military life suited him. He liked the discipline, the clear-cut lines. None of that was Hailey. Yet she was the sexiest, most mix-signaled woman he'd ever met. She'd tell him she didn't date, then plant the hottest kiss with that same mouth. He'd left Hailey at her door, but he craved her sweet-smelling softness the rest of the night.

Next time he wouldn't be forgetting the condoms.

The pilot signaled their approach, and he readied his gear. In orderly fashion each man quietly plunged into the ocean. Cold and bracing. As soon as Nate resurfaced, the distorted sound of some kind of patriotic music blasting from a cheap set of stereo speakers hit his ears. He ground his teeth. The men, searching for the source of the sound, rotated in the water.

But he knew the source. The Sutherland.

People lined the shore once more, but he had to hand it to Hailey, she'd kept her word, but still got her way. Instead of rowdy single women, couples waved to them. The crowd held signs, but they didn't encourage phone calls. No, these signs read "We're proud of our son!" and "Keep up the good work!"

"I think that's my mom," one of the men said, clearly horrified.

For a woman who'd stated she didn't want him in her life, Hailey knew how to make certain he did just that. He found himself smiling in anticipation. Then he quickly propelled forward…should get that two-mile swim started as soon as possible. He had a long night ahead of him.

"WELL, OUR GUESTS HAD their SEALs for the night," announced Rachel as the men swam out of sight. "This went even better than when we had the ladies only. All but two of the parents booked a room. We're almost at capacity."

Hailey nodded, unable to shake her feeling of apprehension as she cleared the tables of napkins and glasses.

Amy pointed to an empty bottle. "Except some of the dads are wanting something other than mojitoes. We'll definitely need more scotch." She then yawned and stretched out on one of the loungers. "All this time on my feet. The B&B business is hard work."

"Tell me about it," Hailey said.

"What's wrong, Hailey?" Rachel asked. "You don't seem excited. We had a great night."

Hailey swiped a tabletop with a cloth. Technically, she'd kept to her agreement with Nate. No distracting women.

"Hailey?"

She shrugged. "I don't know. Inviting the parents seemed like a good idea at the time. A nice alternative to that all-female meat market feel from the other day, but now…"

Rachel gave her sister's hand a squeeze. "Now is the balance sheet. Give that a quick scan, and you won't have any doubts."

And yet, somehow she felt as if she was letting Nate down.

The doorbell rang. "All that use, and the thing still sounds terrible," Hailey grumbled.

"Another couple of SEAL Watch Parties, and we'll be able to afford a whole new announcement system, never mind a new doorbell. You see who it is, I'll take all these glasses to the kitchen."

As Hailey happily avoided kitchen duty as much as possible, she gladly took that deal. Tossing the cloth over her shoulder, she headed for the lobby. With a tug, she swung the wide oak door open wide and was surprised to see a tall, blond man at the threshold. His expression was a combination of worry and anger.

"May I help you?" Hailey asked.

"I'm here for my fiancée. Amy?" he answered.

This must be Jake.

AMY WAS DRAINING THE last of her drink and enjoying the soft cushion of the lounge chair on the terrace. She could stay like this forever. The light gentle breeze, the lull of the ocean as it lapped at the sand all helped to ease her stress. The tension that had been building in her shoulders in the form of tight knots for weeks released more every day. Today was even better. Alone she could enjoy the warm San Diego weather without having to worry about fittings or wedding plans, Jake or diets. Or orgasms.

As long as she didn't let her thoughts drift to the complete mess she'd made of her life, she was totally fine.

"Amy!"

She sprung upright, the muscles lining her back already returning to knots. Her eyes went wide, hoping the sound she'd heard was a trick of too much mojito.

Not a trick. Her stomach pitched and she scrambled to her feet. She was not ready to deal with this. Not yet. She knew Jake was mad, but she'd never wanted to hurt him, would do anything to make him feel better, make up for deserting him like this…but in a few days. Not now. She wasn't ready.

He burst through the door leading from the Tea Room to the terrace. Hailey mouthed, "I'm sorry," and Amy gave her friend a quick nod of understanding. *This* was not her fault.

"Jake," she said, her voice almost breathless. Amy hadn't expected to feel the tightening of her chest when she saw him. She'd practically fallen in love with him the day he'd walked in late to their freshman English class at San Diego State. Now his eyes were filled with pain. Pain she'd caused.

He looked her square in the eye. Dauntless conviction rested in those green depths. "We need to talk."

Amy nodded, knowing there had to be some kind of confrontation. "Let's go to the beach."

Together they took the tiled steps from the terrace to the sand below. Together, but very much apart.

As poor college students, walking the beach had been the only thing they could afford. Since it was free. Along this very shore, they'd talked and dreamed and planned their life together. Tears pricked the back of her eyes.

"When was the last time we were here?" she asked.

Jake shrugged. "I don't know. Feels like a long time ago." He sounded frustrated and a little sad.

"To me, too." They continued to walk in silence, both staring straight ahead. "We shouldn't go too far. There's not much sun left."

He stopped walking and faced her. "Are you ever going to tell me why you left me?"

The hurt in his voice made it hard for her to breathe. The selfishness of what she'd done had fully hit her.

"I had no hint, no clue that anything was wrong," he began. "You never said a word. I think you owe it to me to say something now."

She struggled to find the right words. To make them match her thoughts. "Things haven't felt right in the last few months."

She heard him swallow, watched his Adam's apple move up and down.

"Since we became engaged?" he asked.

"Before that. I was hoping getting married would help that."

Jake made a strangled sound in his throat. "I can't believe this. How could marriage help relationship problems?" he asked, waving a hand in the air.

"You don't understand," she said, looking away, focusing on where the sun met the water's edge in the horizon. As a kid she'd listen to see if she could hear it sizzle.

"I'm trying to understand," he said, drawing her close. "Make me understand."

It felt so good to lay her head on his chest. To feel his arms around her body. *Freeing Your Sexual Self.* The title of the book popped into her mind. Could she be the kind of woman who did the things the book suggested? Amy shivered and felt goose bumps along her arms and the back of her neck.

Jake rested his hands on her shoulder and pushed her away slightly to peer into her eyes. "Are you okay?"

She nodded, not able to find her voice. The warmth from her face spread throughout her body, as the idea of his body moving within her grew more carnal. Her mouth dried. She needed a drink. Maybe she needed him.

His eyes seemed to scan her face, search her eyes. She must have failed at whatever it was he sought because his hands fell to his sides. "Maybe we should head back," he told her, already turning.

Alarm raced through her. That was it? He was ready to let this conversation go so quickly? She was losing him, and suddenly she knew losing Jake was the last thing she wanted. Something strong and urgent forced her to try again. To make him understand. To make herself understand why she did such a crazy thing as leave the one she loved. "All the bridal magazines advise you should never lose the man you're marrying because the wedding has overtaken everything else, but I felt like I'd lost you long before you put that ring on my finger." *The first night he'd taken her to bed.*

"I think I know what you mean."

Her feet wouldn't take another step. "You do?"

"Until you said it just now, I hadn't realized it, but in some ways I think we've just been going through the motions. The steps of life, you know? You graduate from college. You get a job. Then you get an apartment. Finally you get married."

Her stomach began to clench. Jake's words made her feel more like a convenience. Like he didn't really love her. The blow felt almost physical. She hated that damn card right now. "Maybe drawing that fate wasn't such a bad thing after all," she mumbled, feeling bitter.

"Maybe not," he agreed. "It seems as if I've been ignoring things too long."

So what did she do now? Hand the ring over? It felt so final, and suddenly she knew she didn't want final. She didn't want Jake to be feeling the same feelings she'd been having about him.

Back at The Sutherland, Hailey was clearing tables in the Tea Room. She couldn't take her ring off in front of Hailey. It might embarrass him. It would certainly embarrass her.

But Jake surprised her by walking directly to Hailey. "I'd like to book a room," he told her.

Hailey propped her hand on her hip, her flustered gaze zig-zagged between Amy and Jake. "Oh, well, uh…"

"Jake, what are you doing?" Amy asked, shocked. Weren't they breaking up?

He turned to her, a sexy gleam in his beautiful green eyes. A look she'd hadn't spotted in at least six months. "You're setting me free, well, I'm not setting you free." His hands cupped her face. "I love you."

Amy blinked. A rush of emotion made her eyes prickle with unshed tears.

"Put me in the room next to Amy's."

Next to? Her heart beat kicked up a notch.

9

HAILEY SHOULD HAVE BEEN PREPARED. She acknowledged it, yet she was still surprised to open the door and see a not too pleased Nate standing there. Wearing black shorts and a grey polo shirt that matched his eyes, she stopped herself just in time from sucking in a breath at how gorgeous he was.

If fate hadn't already proved what a jerk she could be, dropping into Hailey's lap the perfect specimen of man concluded the matter. He was smart, he knew what was important in life, and could she please stop and admire his body again? Surely he wouldn't mind. Those firm biceps, broad shoulders and trim hips were too cruel.

And she hadn't even gotten to the part where he made her body burn with a mere touch.

"Hailey" was all he said, his voice all business.

She sighed. "Yeah, I know."

Surprise flickered in his eyes as if he'd expected her to play coy or argue. "Noticed that your guys swam through it all. Well done," she told him.

"It was better than just the women, but—"

"Yeah, I know," she said again. She slumped against the doorframe. "We could really, really use the money."

The harsh lines of his face relaxed, and he took the

two steps to stand in front of her. Tower over her, in fact. She looked up, directly into his eyes. He had that straight-from-the-shower appeal to him. Freshly shaven and squeaky clean. There was something very tempting about a squeaky clean man, something inside her wanted to make this man very, *very* dirty.

He reached up and cupped her cheek, his thumb lightly rubbing her chin.

"Would you stop, though, if I asked you to?"

When had she ever thought gray eyes cold? This man's stare burned.

"Yes," she said. And she wouldn't examine why. Wouldn't try to figure out why she was willing to throw away a bundle of cash simply because this man asked her to.

Wait, she knew why. Because she was stupid with men.

And completely dumb about this one.

His gray eyes darkened with pleasure at her answer and something else. Nate leaned forward and he gently kissed the tip of her nose. "Thank you."

Her breath hitched.

He kissed both her closed eyes. "Thank you."

Her stomach hollowed and her heartbeat shifted into high gear.

Then she felt the warmth of his lips on hers. He didn't deepen the kiss, simply moved his mouth against hers. Hailey couldn't breathe, couldn't think. She'd never had a kiss seem so innocent yet affect her so intensely as this soft caress.

"Thank you," he whispered against her lips, then moved away.

She wanted to give him some flip response. Or a

fully confident, "You're welcome." But something about that kiss changed whatever it was building between them. Made it more personal than two people hooking up for mutual pleasure. It scared her a little. She wanted more.

"Maybe I can help. If it's SEALs bringing in the guests, I could ask a few off-duty buddies to stop by."

Her eyes flew open, the dejection of a moment ago evaporating. "Really? Nate, that's perfect. We could have like a speed dating tea thing right in the Tea Room. The women would love it. We could charge a fortune."

His expression grew a little panicky.

"Not what you had in mind?" she asked, not able to hide her excitement.

"They may never speak to me again."

She put a hand on her hip. "Let me make the picture a little clearer. This room will be filled with a lot of SEAL-loving women. Beforehand, I'll feed the men all they can eat of my mom's famous pot roast. It's delicious."

"You make pot roast?" he asked, and she heard the hunger in his voice.

"With new potatoes and lots and lots of corn bread."

"Done."

"Wow, I can't believe how easy that was."

"Yeah, I can't believe I just offered," he said as he made his way toward the front door.

She laughed at his chagrinned expression. This, the fun byplay between them was way more comfortable for her than the charged sexual energy of before.

"By the way, don't think I forgot that you didn't show me your Fate Delivery Card."

He smiled. "All part of the plan."

Of course it was.

"I'll show my card the next time we go out."

Despite the fact that her pulse skipped at the promise in his voice, Hailey felt the need to make it clear once more about her dating status. Regardless of how great his kissing was. Hell, maybe she was reminding herself. "Nate, you know I don't do relationships."

"I remember you *said* you don't do relationships."

"Well, I want you to take my word at face value."

He nodded, but his determined expression told her he didn't believe her. Or that he planned to change her mind.

"Son," someone called from across the lobby.

Nate's face drained of color. There was a man crossing the lobby toward them. Tall, with a full head of dark blond hair, killer smile and grey eyes.

Eyes exactly like Nate's.

"This is your dad?" she managed to choke out.

"That would imply some kind of parental responsibility," Nate said drily. He stiffened as his father stopped to stand right beside him. All military formality. "Sir."

Nate's dad raised his glass, the scotch sloshing within. "You don't have a hug for your dear old pa?"

Nate stuck out his hand. "Good to see you, Jim."

Hailey watched the interaction between the two men who looked so much alike. Nate called his father by his given name, and for the first time didn't seem completely comfortable with a situation. How unlike the warm and caring byplay she'd always shared with her own parents.

"Started calling me Jim when he hit fourteen. Couldn't have a kid crashing my style," Jim told her with a wink. The man oozed the kind of charm that said he'd been fawned over by women since an early age. Getting older hadn't changed his expectations. "Good show out there in the water, son. These ladies sure know how to throw a great party," he said, with a leering wink directed at Hailey.

"Don't," Nate growled.

Jim gave her a quick once over, his gaze staying overly long on her chest. "Got good taste. Just like your old man."

Nate's intake of breath was like a snarl. "You here for the day, sir?" His words were phrased like a question, but sounded more like an order.

Jim raised his hands in surrender. "I won't crash your PI, kid."

"PI?" she asked.

"Stands for public image. Jim's taken to talking in text."

"Hey, Bailey here has a sister. Maybe we could double date."

Hailey's lips twisted into a smile. What do you know? Her big, bad Navy SEAL needed a little saving. "Sorry, I think my sister will be too busy." *Forever.* "Besides," she said as she tucked her arm around Nate's waist, "I like to keep this bad boy all to myself."

Jim raised his glass to his son.

MAYBE YOU'RE NOT SUPPOSED to set him free as in letting him go. Maybe you're supposed to set something in your relationship free, as in exploring.

Could Hailey be right? Had Amy been looking at the card's message all wrong?

Amy decided that yes, she was. She was going up

those stairs. She was going to knock on her fiancé's door and she was going to have her first orgasm.

Um…tomorrow.

No, she really wasn't avoiding the issue…she was setting the stage. Chapter four in Hailey's book had some great suggestions and she'd need a few props to put her plan into action.

The next day, Amy finally worked up the courage to walk inside The Toy Box. She'd been visualizing Jake's body all day long, and was ready for the next chapter. *Undress for His Pleasure—And Yours.*

And that's why she was here now. Earlier on her lunch break, she'd purchased a baby blue, frilly and very very expensive nightie.

But that didn't really seem to fit into the theme of the book. Ducking her head, she returned and scurried to a rack of women's lingerie, each sexier than the last. French Maid, sweet coed, even a referee. But then she spotted a leopard print teddy complete with a thong and naughty cutouts.

Amy could only imagine the shocked look on Jake's face when she revealed herself to him wearing that. She fingered the soft fabric, wanting to prance around his hotel room for his eyes only.

Thinking about the possibility of experiencing her first orgasm Amy threw in a pair of matching leopard print gloves. *I can't believe I'm doing this.* Now to check out.

"We're having a sale on lubes and vibrators," the girl at the register said casually.

Her eyes widened. Amy cleared her throat. "I'm good in that area."

The saleslady took the outfit off the hanger. "I love this set. Have you thought about shoes?"

Amy nearly panicked. She'd taken a major step just walking into this store, but she was definitely ready to get out of here. She shook her head.

"We have a nice selection. I'll show you." With an easy smile, she led Amy to a mirrored area lined with boots and shoes of every color, style and height.

"I think these would go great with the print you chose. They're a six-inch platform, so if you're not used to walking around in heels, we can look at something else."

Platform shoes were the exact opposite of anything she'd ever worn before. Now was the time to go with different.

"I have these in black, silver and gold. Don't let the vamp strap or ankle cuffs throw you, there's a zipper on the back that allows for easy access."

Amy was sure some of what that lady had said would have made sense to someone. When she heard "zipper," the only words out of her mouth were, "If you have them in a seven and a half, I'll take them in black."

The woman smiled. "I'll meet you at the counter."

Now she pulled into the parking area of The Sutherland. She stopped her car right beside Jake's, her heartbeat picking up the pace. She scrambled out of the car, and quickly carried both of the lingerie sets up to her room without being stopped in the foyer, in the stairwell or on the landing that led to her bedroom.

Once inside, Amy arranged each outfit on the top of her bed, which was stupid, because she knew the leopard print was the only choice. And she had to put it on as soon as possible or she'd lose her nerve. She'd tackle her own sexuality. She shimmied out of her work clothes and after a quick shower she slid those thong panties up her thighs.

Okay, not the most comfortable article of clothing she'd ever worn, but what had she expected?

Hopefully, she wouldn't be wearing them long.

A slow smile crossed her face. The gloves were next followed by the teddy. The shoes were even less comfortable than the thong, but a change came over her after zipping them up and standing. Her pulse hammered as she crossed to the mirror. Uncomfortable, but the results…

Not only did they make her legs looks damn good, but they were kind of empowering. For the first time ever, she felt sexy. And that was a very good feeling.

She fluffed up her hair, then donned her navy terrycloth robe. Jake hated the thing, but maybe after tonight he'd gain a new appreciation for it. She lightly knocked on Jake's door, and heard some fumbling around in his room. She smiled.

"Who is it?" he grumbled.

"Amy. Were you asleep?" she asked, trying to keep it light between them. So unlike how their last conversation had gone.

He opened the door a crack, and she watched as he ran his fingers through his rumpled blond hair and down his whiskered face. He looked her up and down.

"Are you okay?" he asked.

She nodded, her heart skipping at the concern in his voice. Even after everything she'd done to embarrass him, he still had her well-being in his thoughts. "I just wanted to talk," she told him, but then opened her robe slightly.

"Amy?" he said.

She pushed the door open, stepped inside, then shut the door firmly behind her. Jake had only occupied the room for a short time, but already it held his scent. She hadn't realized how much she craved breathing him in.

Now she was ready for action. Chapter Seven was all about the strip tease, and she was prepared to try it.

Jake opened his mouth at the same time she let of her robe fall to her feet.

"Wra...wow." His gaze now traveled up and down her body like he couldn't get enough.

A flicker of something she could only describe as feminine power strengthened her resolve. She couldn't stop the smile from curving her lips. Amy liked this feeling.

Jake's hands reached for her, grazed her hips, but she pushed at his shoulders. "Not yet," and she lightly shoved him away.

With a long, lingering glance at her barely covered breasts he walked backwards until his legs hit the high Victorian bed.

She stepped out of the pile of terrycloth pooled at her feet and moved toward him, stopping just out of his reach.

"Amy, before we get any further into this, I think we should discuss—"

"You can't just...run with it? Enjoy it? I plan to strip for you. After that, I'm going to take off all your clothes."

He swallowed.

"Then I'm going to..." *Say it.* "Ride you like a..." *Say it.* "Ride you like a cowgirl."

"Okay." Jake scrambled onto the bed.

She raised a brow? "Who told you to get up on the

bed? If I'm going to strip, don't you think you should be in a chair? You'd like a lap dance, wouldn't you, Jake?"

A lap dance might sound pretty tame to the girls from her wedding shower, but to her it was one of the dirtiest things she could do, and she planned to enjoy the hell out of it.

She sauntered over to the desk, and drew the chair out to the middle of the room. Jake's hands brushed hers. "Here, let me help you with that."

"That's the last time you get to touch me until I say." Earlier, she'd gone on the Internet to find out how to give a lap dance, and that was one of the first principles. "House rules. No touching the dancer."

Amy placed both her hands on his shoulders and thrust downward. Jake settled into the chair, his legs spread. He wore an expression that was a combination of incredulousness and thinking he was one lucky guy.

She planned to *make* him one lucky guy. Loved that he thought himself that way because of her.

"Hands behind your back," she whispered, the scent of the exotic and spicy perfume he'd given to her for her birthday wafted between them.

Jake immediately complied.

She'd downloaded a few sexy songs onto her iphone, which she'd left in the pocket of her robe. Not a smooth move, but maybe she could make this work. She pranced around Jake, drawing her fingers along his arm, across his neck and to the other arm. "Be right back," she said and licked behind his ear.

She quickly grabbed her phone, and soon, sound filled the little room. The mood still wasn't completely right. She *needed* him to see her, but not in full light.

Amy snapped on the bedside lamp and flipped the bright overhead light off. Now this warm soft radiance set the perfect tone.

Dancing had never come naturally to her, although in this instance she was more than determined. She approached Jake with a look in her eyes that she hoped would say, "I plan to give you a good time." Between the V of his legs, she simply moved her hips side to side, and he moaned deep from his chest. As each moment passed, she felt less awkward, more empowered. Amy slinked closer. So near she felt the heat from his thighs.

She began to bend her knees, getting lower and lower. Evidently, this move made a man think of a blowjob. She couldn't imagine Jake ever thinking that since she'd never given him one, but she certainly spotted his reaction. He bulged beneath the zipper of his khakis.

Raising herself, Amy turned and did the same sinking motion with her back to him, only bending over. He groaned at the sight of her thong.

"You are so sexy," he said, his voice rough.

She smiled, for the first time believing that he found her sexy.

Straightening, she backed up. The next suggestion was to caress her own body. *Think of it as slathering on lotion.*

Amy bent forward, giving him a full view of her cleavage. When she reached her ankles, she made lazy circles and strokes up her calves. She brushed her thighs with her fingertips and—

"I want to be doing that so bad."

She glanced up. Oh, hey, this touching herself thing *did* work. Their eyes made contact and what she saw burning in his green depths sent another flood of warmth between her legs. She straightened, taking the opportunity to thrust her breasts at him. Her fingers trailed up her stomach, to touch her skin where the cutouts were, around her breasts, then down her arms. First to remove one leopard print glove then the next. Both landed in his lap.

The next move was to actually do the "lap" part of the lap dance. With slinky moves, she sauntered once more between his legs. She turned and rubbed her backside against his lap. The force of his erection floored her. She'd never felt him so hard. And it was all for her. *Because* of her. She settled against him, giving him more of her weight with a moan-inducing grind.

"Do you like this?" she asked.

"Yes." His reply was a long drawl, like it was difficult for him to get the word out.

"I have more." Her fingers reached for the straps of her teddy, sliding them over her shoulders and down her arms.

Out of the corner of her eye, she spotted his hands move. "No touching," she warned.

Amy lifted off him and backed a few feet away. With the straps no longer a barrier, she peeled the teddy over her breasts and down to her waist. She found Jake's eyes had narrowed to slits.

"Look at me," she said, loving how her nipples hardened as his gaze touched her skin. Amy caressed her breasts then, cupped them and molded them the way Jake did in the dark under the sheet.

It felt good, but it would feel better with his hands on her breasts. Amy approached him once more. She teased his lips with her nipples, but when he opened his mouth, she backed away. "Not yet."

She shimmied the teddy down her legs, standing

before him in only her thong and shoes. "I could make this a full body dance if you were on the bed."

Jake needed no second urging as he leapt out of his chair and was flat on the mattress in seconds. There was that curl of feminine power again that she'd been missing. With a slow gait, she walked to the side of the bed and pushed the thong down her legs. Amy would leave the shoes. Doing Jake with her shoes on sounded just like the kind of naughty thing she'd love to try. So did referring to making love as "doing it."

But what sounded even more wicked was to leave all of Jake's clothes on, just exposing the one part of him she really needed. She lowered her body to his, slowly sliding upwards until she cradled his hardness between her legs. His eyes closed and lines formed across his forehead.

She found the sensitive place above his collarbone and kissed. Then she shifted to the buttons of his shirt. Alternating between a kiss and a lick, she had that whole shirt unbuttoned and his body for her pleasure in no time. Amy gave a quick swipe of her tongue under his bellybutton.

"Keep going," he urged. "This is really getting interesting."

As adventurous as she was prepared to be, Amy was not quite there yet. So she smiled and shook her head.

Jake propped on his elbows to tug the shirt off.

"No," she told him. "Leave it."

Her hands fumbled for just a moment with his belt buckle, but then she had it loose around his waist and his zipper down. Only the black cotton of his boxer briefs separated her hands from his cock. Her hands were impatient as she tugged the material down and she reached inside. He fit perfectly in her hand.

"Pants staying on, too?" he asked.

With a nod, she straddled him. Despite being lovers, there were a lot of things she'd never done. Never initiating sex was one of them. She felt a little awkward, but soon she was teasing herself with the tip of him.

"You're so wet," he said. "I've never felt you so wet."

She squeezed her eyes tight in anticipation.

"I want to taste you," he whispered. The sexy, carnal words nearly did her in right there. They'd never done oral play. The one time Jake had brought it up, she'd been so horrified he'd spent their next date apologizing.

Now she wanted him to taste her, ached for him to. And more, she wanted to feel the hard length of him against her lips. In her mouth.

But the oral stuff would have to wait for another night because the sensation of caressing herself with his penis was exquisite. She positioned him in place and slowly sunk down on him.

When he was fully inside her, he groaned. "You feel so good."

Those were the exact words she wanted to hear. She squeezed her eyes tight again, but this time she was trying to stop a tear from sliding down her cheek. Amy needed to know that she made him feel good. That he wasn't turned off by her sexual needs. The book had said a caring and tender lover would want to hear her desires, and it was right. Jake seemed more sexually excited and charged than she'd ever seen him before.

His hands fisted at his sides, and she felt the struggle within him to let her keep the lead. Amy began to move. The angle, her control of the angle was all new to her, and it felt amazing. She forgot all about books, and mortification and thoughts and just felt. Enjoyed the sweet friction of his body sinking into hers. A tension coiled inside and soon her motions grew erratic. She was so close, so close to something, but she needed a little help.

"Jake. You can touch me now. I *need* it."

With a powerful burst of released his energy, Jake gripped her hips and began to pump inside her. Amy felt him grow even harder. With a gasp, her inner muscles began to clench and she ground against him harder still.

"Now, now now," she urged. "Deeper."

She wanted more. Needed more. And Jake delivered.

Amy couldn't stop the cry that came from some primal part of her body as wave after wave of pure ecstasy hit her.

The sound of their labored breathing filled the room. Amy felt sweaty and relieved and very, very dirty.

"Wow, I've never heard you come so hard," Jake said, his voice sent a trill of sensation down her neck.

Yeah, there was a reason for that. She kissed his cheek. And even though this night was all about talking, some words were better off not spoken.

10

"DID YOU SEE THE LOOKS those two were flashing each other this morning?" Hailey asked as she brought the last of the breakfast dishes in from the Tea Room, where they'd served Amy and Jake this morning.

"It looked to me like she couldn't figure out whether to pounce on him or run away as fast as she could," Rachel replied, putting away cups and saucers.

"She apparently opted for the running away because Jake is out there all by himself."

Rachel gave a quick peek out the door. Jake sat alone in the Tea Room, pushing aside the made-to-order omelet Hailey had worked so hard to create.

"Now *that* is just ridiculous," she said to Rachel. "I mean, I know he's a little confused about life right now, but to waste the delicate fluffiness of the egg like that… It was the kind of omelet mom would have made, and he's ruining it."

Rachel shrugged and took a step back. "Don't look at me, I never turn down food."

Hailey reached behind her to untie the apron strings. "I'm going to talk to him."

"Hailey, maybe that's not such a good idea. It's just an egg."

Hailey almost laughed out loud. "Silly. I'm not going in there to confront him about his omelet. We're going to discover why he's wasting food like that, and work toward a solution together."

Rachel's eyes widened.

Flashing her sister a wink, she looped her apron on the hook by the door. "I'm messing with you."

"Still maybe we should maintain a policy of staying out of our guests' lives."

"It wasn't exactly on purpose, it just sort of happened. Besides, I think I did a pretty good job with Amy. At least there's a little more going on now than just those two arguing. Looks like he's trying to hide a hickey."

Rachel gasped, then she squinted, trying to catch a better glimpse of Jake's neck.

Hailey picked up the coffee pot off the warmer. "Here's what I was thinking we could do for tonight. We'll set up a nice little romantic dinner in the Tea Room…then the champagne and the Fate Delivery Cards will do the rest. Or better yet, we can set the meal up in the Bridal Suite. Cuts out all the work of walking up the stairs to get to the bed."

Rachel shook her head. "Oh, no. I'm not letting those cards anywhere near guests of The Sutherland from now on."

"Don't worry. I'm taking out any of the potentially dangerous cards before I let them loose on that couple."

Rachel gasped. "But that's cheating. I'm not sure we should be messing around with fate like that."

Hailey shrugged. "Maybe fate wants me to 'fix' the cards. Maybe fate put the idea in my head in the first place."

Rachel sighed heavily. "I hate it when you're like this."

Hailey gave her sister a little salute with the coffee pot then headed in Jake's direction.

"Refresher?" she asked.

Jake glanced up, startled. "No, I'm good," he told her.

"The eggs not to your liking?"

The man had the character to look a little guilty. That should prove that Amy had herself a good man. A man who knew good food, and felt remorse when he didn't appreciate the hard work that went into preparing the meal, demonstrated true integrity. He cleared his throat. "No, I—"

"Hey, it's okay. You're having a rough time with it. It's perfectly reasonable you're not hungry." *Sort of.*

He dropped his napkin to the table. "I don't understand how something that could be going so great could fall to shi—er, crap so quickly."

Excellent. Her opening. "What's Amy saying?"

"Other than the first night, she hasn't said much." A touch of red tinted his cheeks, and Hailey could guess that the book she'd given Amy had inspired her to take action that didn't involve a lot of talking. That hickey simply confirmed it. "And I can't get her to open up to me. Really talk."

As the woman who knew exactly what Amy's problems were, Hailey realized she must proceed carefully. She wanted to point Jake in the right direction, but not reveal all of her guest's confidences.

"Amy told me she was raised by her grandparents," she said, aiming for the right conversational tone. "Sometimes I thank my lucky stars I was never born in that generation. We have a lot to be thankful to the women who stood up and paved the way. Our lives have so many more options. And freedoms. Come to think of it, men have benefited in a lot of ways, too. Remember those old black-and-white shows where the couple slept side by side in twin beds? Some of our old records indicated The Sutherland had a few rooms with that set-up."

Jake didn't appear to be particularly uncomfortable with the conversation, the sexual repression problem was clearly Amy's. However, the cluelessness trouble rested squarely on Jake's shoulders. Hailey should probably press further.

"I actually had this one friend who thought her boyfriend would be put off if she showed him her sexual side. They eventually broke up."

Too heavy-handed? Maybe, although something seemed to be spinning inside his head because suddenly Jake started eating. A good sign.

"How could she think that?" he asked after nearly draining his coffee cup.

"You'd be surprised what some women are told about sex and their bodies. That double standard is still alive and well. In fact, I have the perfect book upstairs in my room. You might find it very interesting. Be right back."

Owning Your Bed, Owning Your Orgasm was written by a woman for women, but even the chapter headings should give Jake the right hint. All her life Amy had been given mixed messages about her sexuality and how her worth as a woman was tied into that. Hailey had a feeling Jake was exactly the guy for Amy to work out all her frustrations and confusion with. And on.

Nate looked like a man who could handle something like that. Come to think of it, she had a lot of frustrations…

Focus on Amy and Jake.

Five minutes later, Hailey was charging down the stairs, book in hand when the guest doorbell rang. It had been three days since Hailey had seen or talked to Nate. The fact that she'd noted that it had been three days was a bad sign. Even the Navy hadn't seen fit to grant her a training exercise in the ocean outside The Sutherland, despite the fact that she'd strained her eyes trying to catch a glimpse of a swimmer or a helicopter.

Turned out it was Nate at the door looking tall, and gorgeous and someone she couldn't wait to get her hands on. Her breath caught. He was early.

Definitely her kryptonite.

"Nice book by the way," he said, as he strode through the foyer.

Her gaze slipped to the title in her hand. Perfect. "It's not for me."

"Hey, anytime you want to own your orgasm, I'm your man."

She laughed. "I'll keep that in mind. Is something wrong?" she said. Their SEAL speed-dating night wasn't for several more hours.

"I came to help."

And he ladled on a whole new layer of kryptonite. She would be ignoring that little skip to her heartbeat that thought gave her.

Hours later, the Tea Room was buzzing and Hailey had to marvel at Nate. He'd delivered—boy how he'd delivered. A buffet of men, some dark and handsome, some fair and striking, they all shared that powerfully built swagger of a man who knew how to take care of himself. The women would be thrilled. And better yet— word would get out.

Now those men were polishing off the last of the pot roast and by the compliments she'd received, her mom's recipe still delivered.

Amy, Tori and a few of the other wedding shower guests had come through as well. Over twenty women waited in the lobby. A lobby that would soon have a new sound system thanks to these ladies' money. She could almost jump, Hailey was so excited.

Rachel cleared the dishes in the Tea Room while Hailey stood at the kitchen counter putting the finishing touches on the mojitos they were to serve when she felt, *felt* Nate's presence.

This was super bad.

"Thought I'd stick around for crowd control."

Her lips twisted into a grin as she turned to face him. "Those big, tough Navy SEALs afraid of a few women?"

Nate shuddered. "Terrified."

She laughed out loud. Nate probably wasn't afraid of very much, if anything. Their eyes met and she felt her heart softening. Her resolve to keep things light and uncomplicated dimmed. She swallowed past the tightness in her throat. "Thanks, Nate. I can't tell you how much this means to me. You've gone to a lot of trouble, I can't imagine it was that much of a fair trade."

"I'm getting another date out of this, too." Then the smile faded from his face, and he reached for her hand, his thumb lightly stroking her skin. "I would have done it even without the trade, Hailey. All you had to do was ask."

Then Hailey Sutherland did the craziest thing she'd done in a long while. Overwhelmed by the moment, his gray eyes, and by his words, Hailey reached up and planted her mouth on his.

Nate didn't meet her lips with any sort of surprise or hesitation. His kiss devoured her. And made her stronger, all at the same time. His hands wrapped around her hips and he dragged her close. If he'd hoisted her up on the counter, drew her panties aside and plunged inside, she would have wrapped her legs around his waist. And wouldn't have let him go until he'd given her the pleasure his every look, every word, every kiss had promised her since they'd met.

The buzz coming from the Tea Room broke through her concentration. The click clack of heels and the excited laughter of women poured in from the lobby. With an effort, Hailey pulled away. The sound of their labored breathing filled the large kitchen.

A light sheen of sweat broke out on his forehead, and her stomach tightened, thrilled that her kiss affected this big strong man as much as it had changed the way she planned to deal with Nate. The last time they were together, she'd told him to bring the condoms. Had he? The idea shot a tiny thrill to her heart.

"We'll finish this later," he assured her.

And that's what she was afraid of.

AMY NOTICED SHE HADN'T had a moment to think all evening. The Tea Room was filled with men and women. The numbers were off with more gals than guys, but the time system Hailey had implemented gave each woman a few minutes alone with every SEAL to see if a connection could be made.

As she walked around the room refreshing mojitos,

Amy couldn't help thinking of the connection she'd forged with Jake. The red number circled on her calendar signaling their wedding date loomed still. Well, hadn't they worked out their problems? Sure they hadn't yet had their long overdue conversation, but things were back on track between them, right?

Jake circled the perimeter of the room, picking up empty glasses and scooting in chairs. She loved him so much, she ached with it. When he'd raggedly told her he wanted to taste her, she hadn't been ready.

Tonight she was.

And she was going to taste him. As if he felt her staring at him he glanced up, blinked at the hotness of her look. She gave him a wink. Tonight she would rock his world.

THE NIGHT HAD BEEN an unqualified success. Hailey was relaxing on the terrace, the cool night breeze chasing away the heat from her skin. With Jake, Amy and Nate chipping in, there wasn't even a lot of clean up. What was left could wait until the morning.

Nate dropped onto the chaise lounge beside her. He spread out his long legs, and crossed his arms underneath his head. She expected him to say something, but he didn't. Instead, he joined the silence, staring up at the stars. It was the easiest, most relaxed time she'd ever spent with a man.

And it scared her to death. More than the kiss.

She squeezed her eyes tight and sucked in a breath. After releasing it slowly she rolled over on the lounger to face him. He turned his head, and she was struck by the almost overwhelming urge to touch him. To run her fingers along the line of his nose, the angle of his jaw and the curve of his eyebrow. Hailey wanted to explore his mouth and…

"Thanks for your help tonight, Nate. I really—"

He reached for her hand, stopping her words. Obviously he was as uncomfortable with thank yous as she was. Another thing they had in common—

She wasn't going there.

"What's your weekend look like?" he asked. "I'm ready to call in our date."

Her stomach turned all fluttery at his question. "Amy and Jake should both be gone by Friday, so will a number of the other guests, so it looks like a weekend of painting and trim work for me."

"Any way I could talk you out of that?"

"In a second." The words rushed from her before Hailey realized what she was revealing.

"I'd like to take you up to Anzo-Borrego. Spend the night out there and really see the stars."

"Like camping?"

"And hiking," he added with a nod. "But don't worry, we'll spend the night in Vallecito at one of their tent sites."

This sounded horrific, but then he'd just arranged for a dozen of his buddies to hang out at The Sutherland, and he cleaned up afterwards. "Have I ever given any indication that I'm the kind of girl who likes to rough it?" Because she wanted to identify whatever it was she was doing and put an end to it immediately.

Even in the dark, she could see him eyeing the ruffled, pastel sundress, her painted toenails and dainty shoes. A smile spread across his handsome face and he leaned back against his chair. "No, in fact, I would put you firmly in the girly column." But there wasn't a drop of disappointment in her.

That was a relief. Hailey sighed.

"I'd just like to see you dirty."

With the carnal way he said it, she immediately craved exactly that.

"You can choose the next date," he offered.

"Just so you understand that date will feature a mani, pedi party," she said, her voice a grumble.

Another smooth move by Mr. Peterson. Now he had her agreeing to two dates. Two points for him.

"I'd love to have your feet in my hands," he said in a low, rumbly voice that made her shiver.

"I'm taking a point away from you since you know what a pedicure is," she told him, not being a very good sport.

"What?"

Hailey sat up. "Nate, why are you doing this? Wanting to go out with me? I've told you I'm not at a place where I can do relationships."

The man looked completely unconcerned. In fact, he closed his eyes and took a deep breath. "I'm thinking I can change your mind."

Now if that weren't the sexiest, most irritating thing a man had said to her, she didn't know what it would be. Although whatever Nate did next would probably tie.

"What if I never change my mind?"

The chair squeaked as Nate sat up and dropped his feet to the terrace floor. He stood, reaching for her hands, and helped her stand. The small space between the two chairs didn't leave much room, and the solidness of his chest gently grazed her nipples, making them taut.

He cupped her face and gave her a quick, over-before-she-had-a-chance-to-respond kiss on her lips. But it still tingled. And it still made her warm all over. "Hailey, hopefully I won't be here in San Diego long."

Her stomach clenched. As a result of how much she'd miss him? "Where would you go?"

"Back with my platoon. Overseas. But while I'm here, I want to spend my time with you. You're funny and beautiful and I know we'll be so good together. I can still hear your moans in my head. I want to get you alone, away from here and really be together."

She knew sex between them would be amazing, which was why she'd been avoiding it. Because she'd just want more, more of *him,* and then where would she be? "Maybe we should avoid sex," she hedged.

He dropped his hands and winked. "Then bring your cookies. I liked the peanut butter best."

Sex with her or cookies…and he thought that an even exchange? Her cookies were great, sure, but somehow she felt this was a little insulting. Hailey opened her mouth, but Nate was drawing out a familiar black and red card from his back pocket.

His Fate Delivery Card.

"We talked about showing you this on our next date, but if you want to see it now, here it is. No date attached." Their fingertips brushed as her passed the card to her. "I'm accepting my fate," he said, his warm breath teasing her hair. "You call me if you want to do this." He kissed her temple, then walked down to the beach.

After straightening their chairs, Hailey headed to the Tea Room. *She,* however, needed light to read his card.

She shut and locked the door behind her, then leaned against the wall for extra support. With jittery fingers, she turned the card over. A smile crossed her face as she read *Don't take no for an answer.*

11

AMY LEFT HER DOOR SLIGHTLY AJAR. She'd draped one of the leopard-print gloves over the doorknob to invite Jake into her bed.

The significance of the glove and leaving her door open for him wasn't lost. By inviting him inside her domain, she felt exposed and vulnerable. He'd have all her secrets because tonight she also planned to talk. And more…

By now, she knew just about everything a woman could know about a man. Her man. All except one. How he tasted. After tonight that wouldn't be the case. Once again she acknowledged her plans for tonight weren't such a big deal between lovers, but to her, it was the final reveal.

A knock sounded at her door, and Amy turned, seeing Jake. Her heart contracted. She loved him so much, and she was lucky to have such a guy.

Wait, not lucky, smart. What had the book said? Choice? She was smart to choose such a man to lose her heart to.

Her skin grew achy for his touch. She was anxious to move onto this next step, but still some small part of her wanted to hide something of herself from his eyes. Then he smiled, and every worry, every fear disappeared.

With a purposeful stride, she walked across the room and shut the door firmly behind him. "Remember that first night when I came to your room and you said you wanted to taste me?"

Jake only nodded.

"I want you to. And I want to taste you, too."

She heard him release his breath on a slow exhale. Amy loved it when he made that sound. It meant that she'd surprised him. And turned him on.

"Not freaked out yet?" she asked.

"Never," he told her, his voice rueful.

Amy began to slowly unbutton his shirt, revealing the soft curling hair of his chest, and the flatness of his stomach. He allowed her full rein over his body, and she touched and tasted every part of him.

When her hands found his belt buckle, they began to shake. But she rallied her courage and took control of the metal and leather. Once loose, she shoved his pants down to the floor, followed by his boxer briefs.

The length of him sprang up, and with one promising glance at him, Amy sank to her knees. He was groaning before she had him fully in her mouth. His hands tangled in her hair as she ran her tongue along his shaft and around the head, teasing him. His knees began to shake as she drew him completely into her mouth, and out again. The movement mimicked his when he was in her body.

"Am—" He swallowed. "Amy, how far are you planning to take this?" he asked, his voice sounding raw.

"All the way," she said against his cock.

His hands touched her shoulders. "It's going to kill me to have you stop, but my legs can't take it." He tugged her upward. "To bed."

"Don't think you can handle me?" she asked. Amy had never teased him about sex, and she liked the chagrinned expression that passed across his face.

"Not after three hours on my feet serving restless women drinks and fending off advances. You sure made me work hard to get you into bed."

"But worth it now?"

"Hell, yes." Then Jake apparently found a little extra strength because he swept her into his arms and carried her to the bed. "What was this about me tasting you?"

"Later," she assured him.

"I'll never forget the night your roommate was away and I stayed the night. You told me you didn't do oral. After that, it's all I've been thinking about. Like the forbidden fruit I can't get my mind off of. Let me." His hands trailed up her thighs under her skirt until they reached her panties. "Easy access. You have to wear dresses from now on."

Jake threw up her skirt, then lowered himself between her legs. She wanted to cover her face, to pull him back up, but she didn't. She also wanted to be a woman who could enjoy everything with this man she loved. Amy felt his teeth on the satiny fabric at her hip. He tugged the material down first on one side, then the other. With her panties gone, Jake lifted her legs and tucked them over his shoulders.

His head lowered, and he kissed her gently, drawing her inside his mouth. It was unlike anything she'd ever felt before. Warm and wet and tender. He made a long swipe with his tongue then encircled her, her…clit. "Jake," she whispered, not sure what she wanted to say or ask.

Then he began the tasting part, teasing every part of

her with his tongue. She locked her legs, keeping him in place, and lifting her hips toward him. Her orgasm wasn't a slow buildup like it had been since the first. This climax came out of nowhere, surprising her and making her gasp and call his name. She quaked and trembled and when he sucked her clit once more she came again.

Finally, it was over. She'd never felt so sexually drained. Every muscle lay lax.

"Jake, if you give me a moment, I'll return—"

"If I don't have you right now…"

Amy's eyes flew open. She was going to give him the same kind of pleasure he'd given her, but where she was relaxed, his muscles were visibly strained. She widened her legs and Jake settled himself between them again. "I love you," he said as he entered her.

The rest of the evening they made love, and right before dawn, Amy shared everything about growing up and her fears that he wouldn't want her anymore after the newness of the intimacies they'd shared had worn off.

With a heavy sigh, he folded her into his arms. "Amy, you have to promise me that if we ever have a daughter, you won't let her anywhere near your family. I can't believe how warped you are about sex. Uh, sorry."

She gave him a hug. "No, it's okay."

Pinning her beneath him, Jake's gaze caught hers. "It just kills me that you were taught to be ashamed of your inherent desires. Hell, I *want* you to enjoy sex with me. Demand it anytime. I'm yours for the asking. The taking. Am I making myself clear?"

Amy began to giggle. "Very," she said, feeling

sexual, sensual and very loved. He held her in his arms until her wake-up call from the front desk.

"Let's go home."

Home with Jake. The thought genuinely excited her.

Amy snuggled into the embrace. "Let's go home," she said.

HAILEY FINGERED THE CARD Nate had given her last night. He'd paperclipped his phone number to the back. She lifted up the scrap of paper and read his fate once more.

Don't take no for an answer.

Nate's card wasn't a fate, it was his way of life. A description of his personality. The man didn't need extra help from fate.

Except he would accept a no from her if she chose to give him one. His number. All she had to do was dial the digits and tell him yes. Camping. She sighed. Could he have chosen anything she would have hated more?

No, probably not.

"How long are you going to twiddle that card in your hand?" Rachel asked, carrying a basket of The Sutherland napkins fresh from the dryer.

Hailey wanted to bury her face in the clean fresh scent and forget about making tough decisions. Instead, she dropped the card, washed her hands, and reached for the napkins. Her sister needed help folding.

"If I call him, it changes everything."

"Of course it does," Rachel said, giving her a strange look for stating the obvious.

"I don't want a relationship with him."

"Liar. You may not have observed the looks you toss that man's way, but I have. You can't get enough of him.

Personally, I'd like you to get on with it, so I can stop watching you mope. I don't remember you ever being this moody."

"I'm tired of you giving me such a hard time. I'm in a transitional phase of my life right now."

"No, you're in a won't-make-a-decision-in-life phase because you're afraid of getting hurt. What happened to the girl who left San Diego? She was charged up, ready to hit life with both feet running."

"She came back to San Diego with a broken heart times three."

"Yeah, well, I'm officially putting an end to the moping. A lot of people get their heart broken. A lot of people make mistakes. You're not the only one. I think Nate is a great guy, and you're not exactly making it easy on him. Look at what he's put up with, and yet he's willing to have more."

"I obviously didn't tell you he wants to take me camping this weekend."

Rachel laughed. Hard. "Man, the mental image I have of you is cracking me up. You'll be out there with the bugs, and the dirt and with your antibacterial wipes."

"That proves right there that he doesn't know the first thing about me. How could he expect me to do something like hike? Are there bears in Vallecito Park?"

"No, there's desert," Rachel told her, shaking her head. "Hmm, I actually think this camping thing is kind of sweet."

"You are out of your mind."

"No, listen to me for a minute. He planned your first date all about you. Show that he could fit into your interests. Now he's trying to share what he likes with you, to show you what he's about. Nate must really be into you."

That filled her with excitement and dread. "It's times like these I really miss Mom. I could sure use her advice now."

"I guess we'll have to rely on each other," Rachel said. "And Hailey, I don't need a self-help book to see you're pushing Nate away because he's a man you could really fall in love with."

Her throat tightened and her eyes filled with tears. "I'm not sure I could handle having my heart broken again." Especially since he would be leaving soon.

"Then just make it fun. You said he wants to redeploy. A man like that doesn't necessarily want a relationship either. When you're with him, I see glimpses of my old spunky sister."

Hailey kind of missed her old self, too. Missed the person who left The Sutherland with dreams and hopes and a lot of excitement. Maybe she had been wallowing for too long. "You don't have a sleeping bag or a backpack, do you?"

"Ha, now that's funny. But I'll start a load of sheets in the washer, then we can shop online."

Nothing like shopping to lighten the mood. Or the anticipation of spending time with a sexy man. Hailey dialed.

Nate picked up on the second ring.

"You do realize there's like a million cool things to do in San Diego," she told him.

"Good thing Vallecito is not in San Diego then," he said, and she heard the laughter in his voice, laced with maybe a hint of surprise at her phone call. Pleasant surprise.

"I'm just saying there are other things we could be

doing than camping and hiking." Normally she'd never complain about a date, but she knew Nate was getting a kick from her teasing.

"You're right," he countered. "We'll be geocaching as well."

"Sounds great." Geocaching?

HER NEWLY PURCHASED BACKPACK and sleeping bag waited by the front door. She'd packed plenty of wipes, hand sanitizer and bottled water. Nate told her not to worry about meals, which only made her even more concerned. The man didn't have a good working knowledge around a kitchen and who knew what he thought cooking at a campfire should entail.

She met Rachel at the front door, who'd left early to buy a combo bottle of bug repellant and sun screen. She opened the lid and took a whiff. "I know why bugs stay away. This stuff smells awful. Thinking it might repel Nate, as well."

"Well, then tuck it into your backpack. Bugs might not even be an issue in Vallecito."

The doorbell rang and Rachel gave Hailey a hug. "Here, I'll be mom. Have a good time and be sure to drink plenty of water."

Hailey laughed, nervous and excited, but happy to be looking forward to something.

"Now I'll be me. I slipped in a few packets of condoms, so really have a good time." Then her sister scrambled up the stairs.

Wiping her hands on her new khaki shorts, Hailey reached for the doorknob. If she'd been nervous about the clothes she'd chosen, Nate's very appreciative looks at her bare legs and rugged pink T-shirt chased those concerns away. He looked incredible. The outdoors, and the anticipation of being manly under the sun brought out the sexiness in him.

Hailey expected the hiking boots, and his tan camo shorts, but was surprised to see the pink ballcap in his hands. "This will protect you from the sun," he told her, and placed it on her head.

"Did you buy this specifically for me?"

"Well, I didn't have it hanging around."

She was touched by his gift. Once again she was struck by his effort to take the time and pick out something that she needed, but that she'd also like. His hands rested at her shoulders and she leaned forward. That was all the encouragement the man needed. His lips found hers in a firm heart-stopping kiss. Suddenly, the idea of camping didn't sound too bad.

"This your gear?" he asked, and she loved hearing the anticipation in his voice. "Nice backpack."

"When I spotted the little pink skull and crossbones, I knew this beauty had to be mine."

"Let's go." He easily hoisted her stuff over his shoulder, draping his free arm around her.

They made it to their destination in just under two hours, the terrain becoming dryer and the desert taking over the landscape. As they drove, he asked her about her plans for The Sutherland, and he shared some of his funnier stories about becoming a SEAL and spending most of his time cold, wet and without a lot of sleep.

"So this is going to be a breeze for you?"

"Beats running with a telephone poll."

Nate didn't talk much about his time overseas, but

she heard the pride in his voice when he talked about his fellow SEALs.

"So you never told me why you're teaching," she asked, sipping from one of the bottles of water Nate had packed in an ice chest.

"I was hit by explosives."

"Good Lord, what?" He'd said it so casually, like the way other people mentioned they'd had their bangs trimmed, it caught her completely off guard.

"In the leg."

Hailey had given his muscular legs quite an inspection, and she'd never noticed a scar, although come to think of it, she had spotted him rub his thigh on a few occasions.

"It's higher up," he said quietly, as if he'd read her mind. "In the water I can push through any pain, but I'm point man in my Team, and they can't have someone do land nav when they can't hike."

"But you're okay now?"

"I'm better. My muscles are responding to the physical therapy, but this weekend is going to be my first test."

Hailey wanted to wrap her arms around him, but she sensed the last thing he'd want was to draw anymore attention to himself like this. "So tell me what we're going to search for?"

He raised an eyebrow. "Found out what geocaching is?"

"I looked it up on the Internet."

"But it's not what we're going to search, it's what we're going to find."

Now she was intrigued. "Don't take no for an answer, huh?"

"Got you in that seat beside me, didn't it."

She hid a smile, liking that he didn't want to hear a *no* where she was concerned.

He angled his head toward the dashboard. "There's a printout of what we're looking for in the glove box."

"Are these the coordinates for the GPS?"

He nodded, turning off the main highway. They passed fewer cars now, and the desert seemed never-ending. To the west lay the San Diego mountains, and that was about all she could supply in terms of geography.

"Do you use a lot of GPS when you're deployed?"

"We can, but it's not always something you can count on. Give me a compass and a map and I can get you anywhere."

They entered the campground, and after being assigned a tent site, Nate parked his car near a fire ring. "Like a five-star hotel," he teased.

Desolate was the best word she had to describe it. Sand and brush and more sand and brush.

"You ready to go?" he asked.

"What about the tent?"

"It's a pop up, so we'll have that up in only minutes. I'm anxious to get out there with you and test my leg." He held out a hand, and Hailey eagerly took it. He might just make a camper out of her after all.

Then some kind of flying bug rammed itself against her cheek. Hailey squealed, jumping and trying to get away from the insect. Scratch that whole camper idea.

Nate struck a pose like Superman. "I'll save you from the bug." Then he nibbled where the bug had touched her skin, making her want to shriek for a whole new reason. Nervousness set something off inside her. When they returned, what would he do? Draw her to him? And how would she respond?

Not take no for an answer?

12

AN HOUR AND A HALF later, Hailey was sweaty and no longer squealed when a bug buzzed by. About ten minutes into their hike, Nate put away the GPS and they just enjoyed the scenery together. Although she sensed he ached to challenge himself, he'd taken her on a number of the easier trails. The paths were clearly marked with signs describing the different kinds of cacti and desert wildflowers.

Nate brought her to a tiny oasis and showed her the archeological digs. "This area is filled with fossils."

No longer did she see the bleakness of the sand, but a vibrant desert of amazing vistas filled with hawks flying overhead and even a roadrunner or two. They'd trekked to the top, the view inspiring. Looking down, not seeing another soul, Hailey could image they were the only people on the planet.

"This is one of the few places left in America where you can just pitch a tent in the park."

"Have you ever watched any of those Bizarrely Enough TV programs where they show the petrified remains of missing people? I'm pretty sure pitching a tent below is how it all started."

She'd meant it to be funny. Being hot and sticky, she

needed a little comic relief. But Nate didn't laugh, instead he gently gripped her chin, drawing her toward him. A line formed between Nate's eyebrows, and his gaze grew intense. "I'd never let anything happen to you, Hailey. Never put you in a situation where you could be hurt."

The quiet sincerity, the utter conviction touched some, up-to-this-point shriveled, part of her heart.

And she knew.

Knew Nate would never let anything bad happen to her. It was a strange understanding for her. He was so different from the men in her past. And it was so unexpected to have stumbled upon someone like him.

That's when she decided Nathaniel Peterson was getting lucky that night. Well, as lucky as a man making love in a tent could get.

Hell, he was probably into that.

His thumb caressed her chin, and she leaned into his light caress. She met his gaze, and she nodded. "I know." A brief, sexy smile lifted his lips and she knew he was about to plant one of those amazing kisses on her.

Then she felt the prickling sensation of little tiny legs on her arm. A sensation she'd felt about a million times since leaving Nate's car. The moment lost, Hailey flicked a bug off her arm. She was long past shrieking when one touched her. "I read somewhere that the average person swallows eight spiders in their lifetime. I suspect all those people were campers, and they just skewed the results."

"Beetles kind of taste like apples."

"A. I don't even want to know how you now this. And B. I'm going to pretend that you're joking."

A deep rumble sounded in Nate's chest. He tugged

her closer and looked down into her eyes. She just wanted to keep melting into the steel depths of his. She'd hike, geocache, even sleep in a tent with this guy.

"Don't tell my sister, but I never thought I would enjoy this so much," she admitted, delighting in their water break.

"Your secret is safe with me," he promised, wiping a smudge of dirt from her face.

"Thanks for bringing me, Nate. It's been fun."

"Day's not done yet. We have an appointment at Nineteen hundred."

"What did you just say?"

"Nineteen hundred, er, seven o'clock. Military time. Hard habit to break. It's just adding or subtracting twelve."

"If math is a requirement for dating you, I see why you're single."

He snuck a quick kiss. "Duly noted. No math required. You ready?" he asked.

"Where are we going?"

"We're near Agua Caliente. The state park has two naturally-fed hot springs, like pools. I've been told they're very therapeutic."

"I didn't bring a bathing suit," she said, feeling a rush of disappointment.

"Not a problem."

What did he mean not a problem? Was he suggesting that they go buck naked? Skinny dipping with Nate? Despite the heat, she felt herself grow warmer. "I remembered what a girly girl you are and scheduled a couple's massage in town."

"I fell for that one, didn't I? All right nav man, if there's a day spa somewhere, I expect you to lead me to it."

It took another twenty minutes to hike back to where they'd parked. The air conditioning of Nate's car was heavenly against her hot, dusty skin. Drowsy from the sun, she must have dozed off because the next thing she knew Nate was at her door, gently shaking her awake.

He helped her out of the car, and never let go of her hand as they entered the day spa. The woman behind the desk must see quite a lot of hikers in from the park because she didn't blink at their windblown and dusty appearance. "I booked a couple's massage for Peterson."

The woman scanned her appointment book, then flashed them a smile. "Right this way. There's a sauna shower in the room along with towels and robes."

"Sauna shower?" Nate whispered to her as they walked down the hall.

"How come you didn't know what we were getting?"

"I just asked for the works."

She looped her arm through his. "Now it's my turn to give you an education. Nate, you are going to be a changed man after this. You can have your choice of dry or wet heat. Since the desert was so dry, I'm going wet heat all the way. Over your head will be a rainfall shower, but the best part are the jets that line the wall."

They found their room, the low lights and soft music already relaxing. He popped his head in the stall. "That doesn't look big enough for the two of us."

"This is supposed to be relaxing, not pornographic," she told him playfully. Although a shot of heat pooled between her legs at the idea of showering with this man. Sudsing him all up, then washing it all away.

"How's your leg?" she asked.

He rubbed at his thigh, a move she'd seen him do

often now that she knew what to look for. "Holding its own," he replied, and from the pleased voice, she knew he wasn't just acting tough for her sake.

That might mean he'd be leaving San Diego soon. Hailey hated the pang that thought gave her. She would just have to enjoy him while she could. She busied herself finding a robe and towel and hanging them on the wooden pegs beside the shower. "Okay, first things first. Are you a talker or a shut up and feeler during a massage?"

"I don't know, I've never had one."

"You've never had a massage?"

"No."

"Nate, you have missed out on so much of the truly great things in life."

He squeezed her hand. "Then it's a good thing I hooked up with you."

"For sure. Since you've never done this before, you go first," she said, turning her back to him. "Time to strip."

She heard the sound of his clothes rustling, sliding down his skin and hitting the floor. Hailey held her breath. Knowing that she planned to have sex with him tonight made him undressing now feel all the more intimate. The door opened and closed and she relaxed for a second knowing he couldn't see her reaction to him being naked and so very close.

But him beneath the water raised a lot of questions. Did he shave in the shower or at the sink? Was he a soap or shower gel guy?

Definitely soap. Gel didn't seem manly enough.

Wash his hair first or last? Soon, she planned to discover all that for herself.

After a few moments, the water stopped and she

heard Nate rustle with the towel. Her imagination went into overdrive as she thought about that towel moving across his skin. The way she planned to tonight.

She gave him triple enough time to get dry and in his robe before turning around.

Damn, she should have peeked. Nate hadn't even bothered to get in the robe, simply draping the towel around his hips. If life were fair, that towel would drop. He was something to stare at all right. Little droplets of water held on for dear life onto his chest. She didn't blame them, she'd want to stay perched there forever, too.

On second thought, a few of those droplets began to roll down his chest, over his ribcage and over the flatness of his stomach, roped with muscle. Happy water droplets. Wow, she'd definitely had way too much sun.

"Have I thanked the Navy lately?"

His laugh was deep and sexy and sent shivers all up and down her back.

"You can thank *me* later."

Trying to distract herself from his magnificent physique and how he made her feel, she asked, "How was the shower?"

He raised a brow. "Would have been better with you in there with me. Not as warm as a shower I would have at home, but very refreshing."

"Your turn to turn around."

His gaze rested on her breasts. "Do I have to?"

No. "Yes," she said firmly to him and for herself. A couple's massage was supposed to be a promise of what was to come…not a full blown party in the shower.

"It's a shame," he said, but turned around anyway.

Hailey was out of those clothes and under the water

so fast she didn't have time to change her mind. The water raining over her was just as heavenly as she remembered. Maybe they should install these in a few suites of The Sutherland? She opened the bottle of shower gel, inhaling the floral freshness. The scent was like aromatherapy in a coin-sized dollop, and she felt instantly invigorated. She could have stayed under that water forever, but she had a massage waiting for her.

And a man.

After patting the water off her body, she knotted the towel around her head and reached for the robe.

Nate looked decidedly disappointed by the full coverage of the white terrycloth. Her fingers itched to reach for the ties and slowly pull the material free to expose herself to him. Or better yet…Nate would reach for those ties.

"Now what?" he asked.

"We hop up onto the tables and wait for our masseuses."

He instantly frowned. "You know, when I booked a couple's massage, I thought we'd be doing it to each other."

"Ha, you did not."

"Too bad I returned my Fate Delivery Card."

If the man wanted her hands on his body, he didn't have too long to wait. Their masseuses walked in and Hailey realized Nate was a shut up and feeler. Good to know. He'd closed his eyes, giving her the chance to really look at him. He hadn't shaved in the shower, a light stubble crossed his cheeks and over the cleft of his chin. Hailey didn't mind, she liked the feel of manly skin against hers.

His masseuse began to work and knead on the thickness of his shoulders, and Hailey almost told her to stop. *She* wanted her hands there. To trail along his shoulder blades to smooth the aches away.

She'd never noted how sensual a man's back could be. Just like the rest of Nate, he was lean and lined. The urge to follow the drop of his spine to the small of his back with her tongue had her turning away. She wanted him too much.

But out of the corner of her eye, she saw his hand reach out for hers. She gripped his fingers, and he gave her a tight squeeze. She'd slept with a few men in her day, but none of her experiences ever felt as intimate as holding Nate's hand, knowing they'd soon be touching every part of one another.

After an early dinner in town, Nate drove them to the campsite. As promised, he had the tent up in a matter of minutes. Right now, that two-person red and black canvas looked as inviting as a feather mattress. All that buildup, all this time…she was ready.

He unzipped the front of the tent and she crawled inside. Actually, it wasn't too bad, with plenty of room to stretch out and maneuver. The meshy material of the tent allowed for a breeze, and she began to unroll her sleeping bag.

"Still the girly girl," he said, laughing.

"What gave it away?"

"The fancy deluxe sleeping bag."

"Not something they issue in the Navy? Too bad because when I ordered it online it very specifically mentioned the horizontal quilting made it extra comfy. Way comfier than the bedroll you have."

"That pad won't let a single rock or stick poke me in the night, so we'll see who's more comfortable. Of course, feel free to crawl on over. I'll make room."

She bet he would. "Never thought you'd be with a girly girl, did you?" she teased.

The humor left his eyes. "Actually, no."

Her back straightened.

"Now I can't imagine it any other way."

His words were like a pierce to her heart. Here she was trying to keep things light before he left, but his words, the way he touched her, made her wish for something more than just a fling.

He rubbed his hand through his hair. Looking for the right thing to say? He seemed to think she needed to be romanced. "I want you."

It was the right thing to say. His simple words punched through any remaining doubts.

"I want you, too."

"Then you get me."

With a light groan he finally, *finally,* lowered his head, and her body decided not to take no for an answer. She met his mouth as hungrily as his lips found hers. Everything, from the moment those women prodded her to kiss him on the beach, their picnic, to the massage seemed to be leading to this point.

Ordinarily she liked a man to undress her slowly, but Hailey didn't want to wait another second to get him naked. To be naked with him. Their lips moved in a frenzy. She opened her mouth, and his tongue thrust inside. On her knees, she pulled at the yellow cami she'd changed into at the day spa, their kiss only interrupted when she tugged it over her head.

His hands were everywhere on her body, stroking her back, her bare legs, her arms. "You're so soft," he told her as his fingers trailed down her spine.

Now she wanted that shirt off his back, those shorts off his body and whatever lay beneath. Hailey lost most of her finesse as she yanked at his clothing. At last she could touch and taste him until she got her fill. She loved the sound he made as she ran her tongue down his collarbone, and lower, to suck his nipple into her mouth.

With her cami off, Nate cupped her breasts, teased her nipples with his fingertips. They tightened, and a wave of utter desire slammed straight to her core.

"Pants off," she said, sounding hoarse and very, very aroused.

"Whose?" he asked. "Yours or mine?"

"Both."

His fingers moved to the zipper of her shorts, sliding it downward until the material gaped open. She expected him to slide her clothes down her legs, but instead, he slipped a hand underneath the lace of her panties.

Her breath hitched when he lightly grazed her clit. Then his finger sunk between her legs.

"You're so wet," he said against her temple. "You turn me on so bad."

Good. She wanted to be bad with him. Hailey wanted to feel him, to know what she did to his body. After tugging at the button and the zipper, she pushed his shorts down his thighs.

Nate sucked in a breath, and that wince told her it wasn't from desire.

She glanced up, feeling panicky. "Did I hurt you? That's where you were shot, isn't it?"

He looked embarrassed. "I'm fine, I'm just not used to someone touching me there."

"Sort of like bracing yourself?"

He nodded.

"Then brace yourself." With a push at his shoulders, Nate fell against the downy comfort of her sleeping bag. She tugged his shorts all the way off, then found the scar on his leg. The skin was red, and slightly puckered and she understood why the muscles of his leg tightened on him.

She knew he wouldn't want her to acknowledge his injury, or offer to kiss it and make it all better. Nate was the kind of man who'd want her to accept it and move on. And right now she wanted to move on to his underwear. The black cotton was her only barrier to getting him completely naked.

Hailey could do something sexy, like tug it down with her teeth, but she was just in too much of a hurry. She'd never had a man undressed as quickly as she had Nate. Now he lay totally revealed to her, and she drank him in. She swallowed. Had she thanked the Navy yet? Nate didn't have those big bulky muscles of a bodybuilder; instead he was fit and trim, and very powerful. He'd said he'd never let anything hurt her, and she believed him.

He also wasn't very passive, not content to allow her to gaze at his magnificent body. "Come here," he said and tugged her down until she lay across his chest. In one quick move he had her rolled over onto her back, his mouth at her breasts.

"I can't tell you how many times I've wanted you like this. Those strappy dresses you wear make me want to slide that strip of material down, and do this." He circled her nipple with his tongue, and she felt another flood of warmth between her legs.

"What else?" she asked. Hailey desperately wanted to hear all the ways she made him hot, so she could do them again and again.

"Those flirty little skirts, I can't tell you how many times I wanted to slide my hands up your legs." Nate did exactly that until he reached the soft lace of her panties. His fingers hooked around the material and slowly removed it. "Sometimes this was all I could think of."

"What's the best way to make love in a tent?" she asked.

"I don't know. Let's find out."

"I have condoms in my backpack," she told him, and crawled on all fours to reach it.

Nate groaned behind her. "You are so damn beautiful."

She'd forgotten men typically liked this view.

Seconds after she had the packet in her hand, Nate pulled her backward, her back to his chest, his hands on her breasts. He nuzzled her neck, his tongue making her crazy. She wiggled against him, feeling his hard cock press against her bottom.

"How do you want me?" she asked.

"Every way," he told her, as he took the condom wrapper from her fingers. She turned and watched as he slid the latex in place, then crooked his finger.

With a smile she straddled him, his mouth at her breasts. Gently, she lowered herself, loving how he stretched and filled her. He grabbed her ass, and drew her closer. When he was fully inside her, she wrapped her arms and legs around him.

"Kiss me," he said, and she met his lips forcefully.

The connection she felt to him during the massage couldn't compare. Never had she been this close, this intimate, emotionally, with a man.

At Nate's first push of his hips she moaned, harshly drawing his tongue into her mouth. She ground herself against him, careful to keep her weight off his injured thigh. He lay back, and now she had better leverage, and she planned to make full use of it.

Hailey sank up and down his shaft, and he groaned. "This is better than I'd ever imagined."

She loved that he'd imagined what she'd thought about so often.

"One more," he said and rolled her to her back.

She looped her feet together behind his back and jerked him to her. His thrusts were powerful and fierce, and Hailey couldn't get enough. "Harder," she urged. Nate gave her exactly what she asked for.

Her every nerve ending felt on fire. The force of him against her finally drove her over the edge. She used her legs, her arms to urge him on. "Nate," she cried out as she reached her peak.

He grew rock hard inside her, his every muscle tightening and clenching. He groaned out her name as he came. Hailey smiled at the sound. She could listen to that all day.

Nate collapsed to his side, tucking her against his chest.

"I changed my mind. This beats your cookies hands down."

13

WHY WAS IT ALWAYS easier to tell a man secrets in the middle of the night? It probably had something to do with resting her head in the crook of his shoulder after making love. The reassuring lull of his heartbeat. The quiet moments of sharing as she ran her finger along his skin all enveloped her in one big tempting urge.

"You know that phase where you think members of the opposite sex are gross?" she asked.

He dropped a kiss on her nose. "Yeah, in fourth grade I thought girls were yucky." He even added a faux shudder.

She gave his arm a playful push. "Well, I never went through that stage. I always liked boys." She'd had at least six self-help books tell her she'd missed out on some elusive yet important socializing factor that helped women know the good men from the bad.

She leaned on her arm, loving the way the light from the lantern played on his face, deepened the cleft in his chin. "That's why you're dangerous."

His lips turned up at the corners. "I'm irresistible, am I?"

Pretty much, yes. Instead of telling him that, she shoved at his shoulder. "Be serious. You can't charm your way around being harmful to women."

"I hate the word charm," Nate said, his smile waning.

She took a deep breath, was ready to admit why she needed to keep him at a distance. She remembered his dad. The tension between them. His dad was full of charm; now she understood why Nate hated the word applied to him. "You know how I said I didn't do relationships?"

"How could I have forgotten? You reminded me of it every time you kissed me."

"*I* kissed *you?*" she asked, incredulous.

"All the time." Then he leaned forward. "But I didn't mind," he whispered in her ear.

Somehow his playful attitude made this late-night confession easier. "I like you. A lot. I want to spend time with you, get to know you better. And then I'll really be in trouble."

He twined his fingers through hers. "You're saying it like that's a bad thing."

Hailey nodded. "It is. You see, I follow a very predictable pattern. I'll take your interests for mine, come to depend on you, and then where will I be when you leave?"

"Where am I going?" he asked, placing a kiss on her cheek.

"You told me yourself you couldn't wait to rejoin your team…wherever."

"That doesn't mean—"

"Don't say it." Whatever pacifying thing that was about to come out of his mouth she didn't want to hear it. It would make leaving him all the more difficult.

His expression grew concerned. "Why is it so hard for you to believe that I'll stick around?"

Reaching around him she snagged her T-shirt, and slipped it over her head. There should be a warning about sharing secrets in the night; all the sloshy romantic feelings would be lost. "Because first, you're a man, and second, take a good look at yourself, Nate. Look at your job, you're itching to go overseas now. You're practically *designed* not to stick around."

"The job moves around a lot, yeah, but that doesn't mean I don't want to come back to you. A guy would be an idiot to *want* to leave you behind."

Her throat tightened, and Hailey closed her eyes. It would be so easy to believe. So easy to allow herself to get sucked in by his gray eyes, easy manner and gentle words. His *charm.* But she wouldn't. Because Hailey couldn't trust her feelings. Her feelings had gotten her into a lot of trouble in the past. Even now they were telling her that a long-distance relationship would work. Go ahead and let yourself move beyond just a fling.

This was the lesson she was supposed to have learned. Feelings messed up her life.

Usually, in a situation like this, with Nate half naked and making her beautiful promises, she'd be lobbing herself into his arms and telling him that she loved him. And maybe a Fate Delivery Card had delivered him into her arms, but it still didn't change the fact that her instincts were off where men were concerned.

So she wouldn't be falling in love, but she would be falling in fling. Friends with benefits. Platonic sex.

Nate was an unselfish lover who made her feel incredibly good in and out of bed. So, yeah, she'd enjoy him while he was around, be sad when he left, but his life wouldn't become hers.

Hailey cupped Nate's face. "Make love to me, now."

STRIKING THE TENT Sunday morning and clearing camp wasn't as easy as setting it up.

"It never is," Nate drawled, pouring the last of the water on the fire. This morning he'd made them something called scramblesmash, which was basically eggs, cheese, peppers and onions all cooked over an open fire. And it was delicious.

They had an easy drive into the city, and Nate helped carry her backpack and sleeping bag into The Sutherland. And here was where the awkwardness started. Usually, she'd invite her man inside, offer to share her bed for the evening…but that was relationship territory, and as he liked to tease her, she'd told him she didn't do relationships plenty of times.

Nor was she going to hint around to find out when she'd see him again. From now on when she wanted to go out with him, she'd call. Not wait around for him to dial.

The lobby couldn't have looked any less welcoming, so she turned to her SEAL instead. "I had a great time, Nate."

A slow, sexy smile found his lips, and she couldn't help responding to it.

"Me, too," he told her. Then his smile wavered. He scrubbed his hand down his face. "We'll be out doing drills for the next three days, so I won't be in touch."

"I understand." See? It was already working out great. Already the intense intimacy they shared this weekend was cooling. Him going away fit perfectly into her comfort zone.

Brave words. Stick with them.

"I'll call you when I get back."

He might…he might not. It was all good. *She wasn't even a proficient liar.* But she had to do something to distance herself. Fling not feelings.

With a lingering glance at her lips, Nate then turned and walked out. Her breath released in a large exhale. The clamoring footsteps down the stairwell let her know Rachel had been waiting to pounce.

"So, how was it?" she asked before even taking the last step.

"It was good."

Rachel crossed her arms against her chest. "Good?" she asked, with a lift of her eyebrow.

Hailey felt the heat of a flush on her cheeks.

"That's what I thought," Rachel said after spotting Hailey's obvious reaction. "Just tell me one thing, am I going to have to buy a new box of condoms?"

With a laugh Hailey nodded, and Rachel gave her a high five. "Amy called after you left. She'd like us to host the wedding as well as the reception afterwards. I couldn't turn them down."

It probably would come to no surprise that a woman who'd been engaged three times loved weddings. Truthfully, she didn't really need a lot of convincing. The prep work might keep her mind from straying to Nate. "We've never hosted anything that big."

"We have to start sometime. I've already made a to-do list. Why don't you look it over while I call Amy back. She has to get the information to the printers for the invitations."

Yes, invitations were important. She'd recycled over four hundred of them. Luckily she'd ended it with Fiancé Failure Number Three before placing her order.

Hailey quickly scanned the list, noting a lot of carpentry. Not her strong point. Her thoughts drifted to Nate. Was he good with a hammer?

No. Not going there. That was relationship thinking, and she wasn't having it.

NATE WAS BACK AT BASE at 0500. He smiled, remembering Hailey's remark about him still being single and attributing it to the way he told time. Thoughts of his single status never popped into his head. He'd dated women, but they'd never lasted through a deployment. The idea of a woman waiting for him back home sounded like a burden. What did he have to offer, but a string of lonely nights? Nate was born to be a SEAL, and his career came first.

Only now he wondered if he had room to add one more thing.

The dull ache in his thigh taunted him. What was after his time with the Teams? Still, he had years to go before his body couldn't meet the physical demands, and he gave up his place to younger men, but that time would come eventually. Would he start looking for someone to share his life then? It sounded ridiculous. He guaranteed that no one like Hailey, who baked him cookies and looked at him as if she couldn't wait to rip his shirt off, would be hanging around that long.

"Nate."

He turned from where he was preparing his gear to see Riley, charging toward him. "Just wanted to give you a heads-up, a couple of the guys who couldn't make that dating thing at The Sutherland are looking for you. They want to know when the next one is."

And here he'd thought he'd pulled every favor with

his buddies to get them there. Apparently they wanted more. He couldn't wait to tell Hailey and watch her eyes light up. Those three days loomed large now.

"I'll pass along the word," he said.

"I've got a date tonight, and another tomorrow."

"Doesn't sound like it's the same girl."

Riley shook his head. "When you're in demand, you gotta give the women what they want."

"Sounds like dangerous living."

"Good thing I'm a SEAL."

Nate laughed as Riley walked away. Funny, there was a time when he felt much the same way as Riley. He kept things light with women, always after a good time.

Hailey was a good time, but she was so much more. She made him laugh, she made him hot and she made him think. And it didn't scare the hell out of him that he wanted to discover how much more she was to him.

OF COURSE, TELLING HER thoughts to stay away from Nate was a lot easier in theory than it was in practice. Hailey swiped her lemon oil filled cloth across the wainscoting of lobby walls. "I think the ceiling color looks awful. Maybe we should repaint."

Rachel heaved a dramatic sigh. "I'll be glad when Nate gets back. Maybe you won't be so gripey."

"I'm not gripey," she snapped at her sister.

"Okay, you just keep believing that. Remember when I said I hated seeing you all mopey? I'm taking it back. I'd way rather deal with mopegirl than Ms. Nothingisright."

Hailey stopped wiping the wall. So far her fling idea

wasn't working out so well. She couldn't stop thinking of Nate, and that made her mad. Really angry. With herself, at Nate—both of them.

She turned and faced her sister. "Isn't there some saying that as soon as you decide love sucks, it comes to bite you in the ass?"

Rachel was clearly trying to hide a smile. That made Hailey even more irritated. "I don't know if that's the exact wording…"

"Well, it should be." She'd been resisting the idea of Nate for so long, she'd almost missed out on how good it felt to fall in love with someone.

"I'm glad you're finally admitting it. That whole fling thing sounded pretty desperate."

"But I don't want this. I don't want to care about him, and focus on him all the time. I'm finally getting things back to normal in my life."

"I hate to break it to you, but they weren't that normal."

"How about more normal for me?" Hailey slumped on the stairs. "I should never have taken that card."

"Really?" Rachel asked. "I know you're feeling rough, but would you rather have never met Nate at all?"

Her mind flashed to him pulling that injured man onto the beach, racing down the beach with a kite blowing in the breeze behind them, teasing her about revealing his card, laying across from her at the day spa, making love to her in the tent. "No."

"I'm glad you said that because I think that's Nate coming up the walk right now."

"Now?" Hailey surged to her feet. She looked terrible. Her hair was wrapped in a lavender bandana and she was covered in cleaning products. They'd left the doors and windows open for some air circulation so all she had to do was face the doorway and watch him walk through.

Had it only been three days? It felt much, much longer, and her heart beat faster at the sight of him. Nate appeared exhausted. Lines fanned from his eyes, and his shoulders drooped. As an instructor he did almost everything his men did, and whatever it was they'd done had nothing to do with sleeping for the last three days.

Her irritation and frustration with falling in love with this man faded when she saw him smile and a fire behind the steel eyes of his.

"I'll just, uhm, be in the kitchen," Rachel said, leaving them alone.

How could a man look so good? She had no idea. She allowed herself to drink him in with her eyes. Hailey didn't want to seem too anxious, but she raced across the room, ladylike, of course, but she wanted him. Right now.

"You seem tired," she said, stroking his pale cheek.

"And when you look at me like you're doing right now, all I want to do is find the nearest bed as fast as I can and stay there." He hauled her up his body, smelling of soap and the outdoors.

"What do you know, we just happen to have quite a few beds upstairs."

"Show me the way."

After seventy-two long hours she was hungry for him. She didn't want a slow, explorative experience. She wanted him with the desperation of a woman who'd just realized she loved the man she was with and their time together surely would be short. Their clothes were off the moment her bedroom door closed behind them. She tugged his head down to her breasts, arching toward him.

His mouth circled her breasts, finding her nipple and sucking. She ran her tongue over his ear and down the side of his neck. With a groan he hoisted her against the wall, his cock between her legs.

"I want this to be good, but I'm so hot for you, Hailey," he said roughly, his lips at her collarbone.

And that's how she wanted it. Against the wall and fierce. She wrapped her legs around his waist, feeling his erection already probing her.

He groaned. "You're killing me, Hailey. I've got to get a condom."

She released him. "Just come back. Quick."

Nate flashed her a sexy look that told her all she needed to know. He dug around in his wallet, making impatient sounds and she smiled. Then he was back, raising her to his waist, and she locked her feet behind him. With one stroke he was in her, and her moan matched his.

"Open your eyes," he insisted.

Her lids drifted open, and her gaze collided into the warmth of his. He pulled away and thrust again, his eyes never breaking contact with her. "You feel so good," she told him. "You make me feel so good."

Her words must have triggered something deep inside him because his shoulders tensed. "I can't hold out any longer."

"Then go."

Afterward, they lay on the bed, Nate drawing lazy

circles on her arm and staring at her wall. "What would you say that color is?" he asked.

"When I picked the sample out at the store, they told me it was called blush."

With her head on his chest, she felt and heard him laugh. "I knew it had to be something like that. Can I ask you another question? What's with all the horse stuff?"

Hailey rolled over and smiled. "You remember our talks about me being a girly girl?"

"I see the evidence all around me." There were a lot of things here leftover from her childhood.

"Well, one of the side effects is a love of all things equine. I have half a dozen notebooks filled with nothing but drawings I made of horses."

"Just horses?"

She shrugged. "Some were ponies."

He chuckled softly, hugging her closer.

"Okay, now I get to ask you a question."

"Shoot," he said, looping his arms behind his head.

"I'm trying to figure out what's wrong with you. I mean what is your issue?"

"My issue?" he asked, his brows drawing together in confusion.

She began twisting the fitted sheet with her fingers. "Yeah, what is it that you want from me? What makes you want to be with me? My first fiancé wanted me because—"

His hands stilled hers. "I don't want to discuss who you were with before me. They let you go, so believe me they were all idiots."

Hailey battled a smile. Everything inside her screamed now was not the time for honesty. No time was good, in fact, but she had to run with this. "I worry about who I choose. The engagement thing, it's there. It will always be there."

"How about, those guys just weren't right for you. I am." Nate peered into her eyes, his gaze a steely gray. "I want to be with you because I like you."

"Why are you still single?"

"I hadn't met you yet."

The perfect answer.

AFTER A LONG POWER NAP, Nate followed Hailey downstairs, and for the price of spaghetti and meatballs and oatmeal cookies, The Sutherland had neatly clean baseboards. Nate turned out to be handy with a hammer, and fixed a few that were loose.

That evening, she mixed him a mojito and they lazed together out on the terrace.

"This is one of the worst things you've ever served me," he told her after a single sip.

She raised a brow. "One of?"

He raised his hands in surrender. "Okay, okay. The only bad thing."

"That's better. Would you like a beer?"

Nate shook his head. "No, I have to drive back to my apartment."

Hailey stared out into the surf, knowing she was about to make that next big step. "You could always stay here for the night."

He cut her a sideways glance. "I have to get up pretty early in the morning," he warned.

She nodded, still not taking her eyes from the beach. "Doable," she told him.

Nate surged to his feet, drawing her up with him. "In that case, forget the beer, let's go to bed."

The next two weeks followed a very similar pattern. On his days off, Nate was at The Sutherland helping them with all the little things that needed to be done before the wedding. Amy and Jake joined them. For meals, they sampled Rachel's creations. Her sister had a lot of plans for a new menu, most of them fantastic. For the first time in a long time, she felt hopeful about the future.

On those evenings when Nate didn't have to get up so early the next morning, he stayed over. Sometimes he made tender love to her. Other times it was as fast and wild as that first time in her bedroom. After the initial night when her invite had come out of the blue, Nate had always brought his beat-up old Duffel bag.

When she opened the door to him, her eyes always strayed to his hand to see if he clutched it. She'd grown to love seeing that Duffel bag because she knew her night would be filled with the pleasure only he could give her.

That was why she was so surprised to see what he'd left on her dresser. Panic burned in her chest. "Rachel," she called. "Come quick."

"What? What?" Rachel asked, rushing into the room. "At some point you're going to have to learn how to take care of the spider yourself."

"No, look!"

"What?"

Impatiently, she pointed to her dresser. "Don't you see it? It's his comb. He left it here."

Rachel propped her hand on her hip. "What's the big deal? You're having sex with him, right? That *is* Nate Peterson I see leaving sometimes in the morning?"

"Well, yeah, but that's in a platonic, uh, way…"

Rachel began to laugh. "Did you almost tell me you're having platonic sex? I mean, that sounded like what you were about to say, but even you can't be *that* delusional."

Hailey flopped onto the bed clutching his comb to her chest. "Oh, Rachel, I'm in trouble here. Everything I'm feeling I don't trust. I have to end this right now."

14

NATE FINALLY HAD THE ORDERS he'd been waiting for. In less than a month he'd be back in the Teams, this time out in the Indian Ocean. Strange, Nate always knew where he belonged, how he fit in this world, but with Hailey in his life things had changed. She'd changed him.

"I heard the good news," Riley said. "Got my orders, too. I'll be sad to kiss all the ladies goodbye, but it's where I belong."

"I know what you mean," Nate replied.

"Doesn't sound like it. All those free meals at The Sutherland softening you up?"

Nate shut his locker with enough force to be considered a slam. "No."

Riley held up his hands, backing off.

"Sorry," Nate mumbled. He was acting like a jerk.

"No problem. I've seen this before. Have you dirt dived her yet?"

Nate didn't bother pretending he didn't understand Riley's meaning. Twelve men saw her kiss him on the beach, so word got around when he spent less time in the weight room. No, he hadn't dirt dived her. SEALs planned, tested and retested every action, every drill, so that it would become second nature. With Hailey, he hadn't planned his next step. He couldn't even anticipate her reaction to his wanting more. It was a stretch to bring his Duffle bag that first time. Nate shook his head.

"Figure something out without making the ladies mad, would you? I don't want to miss out on pork chop night." Riley's laughter echoed down the hallway.

He was kind of partial to Hailey's pork chops, too. He was partial about everything where that woman was concerned. He'd learned to tread carefully when it came to the relationship they *weren't* having, but his orders created a sure problem.

He loved her. It wasn't something that he'd planned, but he liked it. Now he wanted things differently in his life, things that included her. And today was the time to act.

HAILEY WAS STAPLING THE last bit of fabric to one of the high-back chairs she'd pulled out of storage. As furniture goes, it was sound, just needed to be reupholstered. She'd saved their budget a cool two-thousand bucks with that afternoon's work. She dusted off her knees at the sound of the doorbell. The staple gun slipped from her fingers because she knew Nate would be on the other side of that door.

And he wouldn't like to hear what she had to tell him. She ignored how good he looked as she opened the door. Instead, she pulled the comb from her back pocket, and slapped it in his hand.

"You found it," he said, following her into the foyer. He tossed the black plastic in the general direction of where he'd already dropped his Duffle bag.

She closed her eyes and felt her chest tighten. That bag almost did her in. Knowing she could spend one last night in his arms loomed so tempting. But it wasn't fair to him or to her. Hailey opened her eyes, and faced him with resolve. "You can't leave your stuff here, Nate. It's not like that…it's not like that between us."

Nate squared his jaw, obviously full of resolve himself. *Don't take no for an answer.* Fate had given him the wrong card.

"How is it between us, Hailey?" he asked.

His voice sounded odd. Cold. She also noted a hint of a challenge. "We're just friends," she said with a shrug.

"Friends who make love?"

She shook her head. "Friends who have sex."

He scrubbed a hand down his face. "That's crap, and you know it."

Now she was mad. "I told you right from the beginning that I didn't do—"

"Do relationships," he finished for her. "Yeah, I know. You've told me a million times."

"You obviously weren't paying attention."

"How could I over all the mixed signals you've been sending my way." Nate stormed toward her, dragged her tight against his body. "You make love to me like a woman who can't get enough." She felt his every straining muscle. His erection almost made her cave. "Tell me you don't want me, Hailey."

She met his eyes, saw the raw intensity, the raw emotion he felt for her in those depths.

"I love you, Hailey. That's all you need to know. I love you."

Her eyes filled with tears, and she turned her head

away. "I don't want you to love me." It made it harder to say since she knew she loved him, too.

He released her carefully. "If it's any consolation, I don't want to love you, either."

She gasped, swiping at her cheek.

"Actually, it's not true. I'm glad I love you, Hailey, even though you don't make sense a lot of the time."

Something that sounded similar to a sputter came out of her mouth.

"But I'll tell you what does make a lot of sense. You and me. At first I thought I wanted what you wanted. A quick, fun fling. Someone to spend my time with between deployments like every other woman I've had in my life. But that all changed because I fell in love with you."

"How do you know you actually love me? That it's not the heat of the moment?" Three other men had told her they loved her, too. But none of them had…not really. She couldn't bear it if Nate did the same. He was too special. She loved him too much.

"Because I've never been in love before."

"Never?" she asked, shocked.

He shrugged as if it was no big deal. "I was never looking for it. You saw my dad. The kind of man he is. I didn't want to be like him."

"All guys want to be like him. A different woman every night," she challenged.

"Maybe hearing my mom cry so much made me not want to be like all the *guys*."

And here he was stuck with her. With her past relationships, she was more like his dad. Fate had its irony too, that was for sure.

He cupped her face. "I wasn't looking for love, but you

made me realize how lonely my life has become. I know it's probably not the life you imagined, Hailey, but we have something special, so I'm asking you to wait for me."

"Wait for you? What do you mean?"

"I got my orders. I'm shipping out."

"When?" she asked, her throat feeling raw.

"End of the month."

Hailey tugged away from his grasp and wrapped her arms around her waist. "I'm happy for you."

"You're not going to wait for me, are you?" he asked slowly, like he needed to hear her say the words.

Hailey shook her head.

"Why? I know you have feelings for me, Hailey."

"You're right." She couldn't lie to him to make this easier on herself. She owed him more than that. "I do have feelings for you."

"Then what's the problem?"

"I don't trust those feelings. After my last breakup I left my job and my home in Dallas, but it was more like running away. I can't risk my heart again."

He gently wiped a tear away from her cheek. "I told you I'd never let anything hurt you."

Hailey gripped his hand, needing his warmth even though she was being selfish. "You wouldn't mean to. I'm sure right now your intentions are all good. But so were theirs, and look where it got me."

"So that's it? You're giving up?" he asked, his hand falling from her face.

"I think this is just the way it has to be."

He looked like a man who wanted to argue with her. To try to convince her everything would work out. As a SEAL he was used to making things work his way.

Nate drew her chin up toward him and kissed her. His warm lips soft against hers. It was a goodbye kiss.

She watched as he turned away from her, reached for his Duffle bag and walked out of her life. Hailey almost called him back. Almost ran toward the door so she could block his exit. Instead, she stood planted to the hardwood floor of the foyer, praying she hadn't made a mistake.

TWO HOURS LATER, Hailey joined Rachel in the kitchen where her sister was shelling peas for their dinner. "Where's Nate?" she asked. "I thought he'd be joining us. I bought chocolate chips so you could make him more cookies."

"He got his orders. He's leaving." Hailey felt dead inside.

Rachel's face was a picture of sisterly outrage. "So that's it? He's done with you? That jerk."

Hailey swallowed over the lump in her throat. "No, he, uh, he asked me to wait for him."

"Well, that's just great. You're supposed to wait on him and he gives you nothing?"

"He told me he loved me. I think he would have asked me to marry him if I'd given him the chance." How she'd wanted to give him that chance.

Rachel huffed so hard her bangs blew. "Big sis, you're making it really hard to be on your side here. So what did you do?"

"I told him it was over."

Rachel tossed the remaining peas in the strainer. "I knew this was going to happen. Have you ever thought that maybe one day you're going to push the wrong someone away, and they might stay pushed?"

Fighting tears, Hailey busied herself wiping the kitchen counter where water had splashed. "Easier for them not to break my heart that way."

"Not that you're interested in my opinion, but I think this is bad. Nate is different from all those other guys you dated."

"How so?" she asked, trying not to sound defensive.

"First off, he doesn't want anything from you other than to be with you. To share his life with him."

Hailey sighed heavily. "What's the point of bringing this up?"

"Because besides being total losers, not one of your other guys ever made you truly happy. Nate did. He wanted to. *That's* what makes him different."

THE NEXT WEEKS PASSED in a blur of wedding preparations. Amy's complete happiness only highlighted how miserable Hailey had become. At some point she realized she hoped Nate would ignore what she'd told him and contact her anyway. But he wasn't like that. He respected her wishes. Ugh.

Stop thinking about him.

"Hey, I hope it's not awkward for you, but Jake invited Nate to the wedding. They became friends when Jake and I were working here," Amy said.

Hailey gave her a blasé shrug. "No, it's fine."

But it wasn't fine. She couldn't walk along the beach without seeing Nate pull a man there to safety.

She couldn't eat in her kitchen without thinking how easy it was to get him to see things her way, after she placed a plate of cookies in front of him. Even the lobby and foyer had his touches, from opening the front door and seeing his smiling face, to the baseboards he'd helped repair.

And her bedroom? There the memories were the worst.

The idea of sleeping in one of the guest bedrooms popped into her mind, but could she ever forget what it was like to snuggle next to Nate, no matter which bed she was in. Besides, with their increased bookings, they didn't have a lot of rooms to spare.

Three failed engagements, yet none of them ever devastated her the way asking Nate to leave her life had.

She was in love with him.

Hailey breathed in the feeling, loving that she could finally admit it to herself. Wanted to shout it to her sister. Whisper it in his ear.

Only she'd hurt him pretty badly. It didn't take a lot of experience with men to know that when one of them told you he loved you, and you told him to go away, it would be tough to win him back.

Shoving off her bed, Hailey marched down the stairs and into the kitchen. There on the desk lay the box of Fate Delivery Cards she'd vowed to burn at least a dozen times, but never had. With trembling fingers she drew every card until she found the one she really wanted. His card.

Don't take no for an answer.

THE MORNING OF THE WEDDING was a typical San Diego beauty. The Sutherland was a bustle of activity the way Hailey remembered it growing up. The florists arrived on time with gorgeous centerpieces for every table. The Tea Room had never looked better. Bows and greenery wound around the railing on the trellis and the rented chairs fit perfectly on the terrace. An arch of flowers marked where the bride and groom would share their vows and candles perched nearby. It was simply stunning. Rachel draped her arm over Hailey's shoulder. "Mom would be proud."

Hailey nodded. "I think she would be, too."

"Don't worry about Nate. In fact, I think you should look at this as closure. One more time to see him, and then it's over. You'll never have to lay eyes on him again," Rachel said. After stating her opinion that she was a fool to push Nate away, her sister had stood by her faithfully the way she always had.

Hailey gave her sister a reassuring smile, but knew she couldn't fully agree. This time when she saw him, she'd be at a disadvantage. Nate had something she wanted, him, and she doubted he'd still be too interested in her after everything she'd said. The doorbell rang.

"Our first guests!" her sister excitedly announced.

Hailey, however, was filled with trepidation.

The guests seemed to arrive in clumps, and after escorting them through the lobby and to the Tea Room and terrace, Jake's groomsmen took over with the seating. And Nate came alone. She'd seen the man in a wetsuit, T-shirt and shorts, and naked, but he was *amazing* in a suit. What was it about a tie that made her want to pluck at the knot and tug that thing loose?

He greeted her sister with a kiss to the cheek, but seemed reluctant to face her.

Remember the card. Remember the card.

Finally, he turned toward her and Hailey met his

gaze. She heard his sharp intake of breath and felt a tiny spark of hope. His gaze ran up and down her body. He wanted her, and she went weak inside. *Yes.* Maybe, just maybe she could pull it off.

"Hailey," he said, his tone impersonal.

"Nate."

Rachel had offered to escort him to the Tea Room, but Hailey knew she wanted him to herself. "Follow me," she told him.

He matched her steps through the lobby, both of them silent.

"How have you been?" she asked, knowing he probably wouldn't initiate any conversation.

"Fine."

"I'm glad."

"You?" he asked.

"Fine." *Lie.*

"I'm glad." Ugh, this conversation was horrible. And painful. She didn't have much time before she had to turn him over to someone else. Hailey cleared her throat. "I hope you don't mind, but would you stand in the back with me? I, uh…need help with something."

Okay, as excuses went, it could be plausible, and very doable as it was so off the cuff. Nate nodded, and she flashed him a quick smile before she had to return to the front door. The final guests filed in and Hailey and her sister headed for the Tea Room.

"Nate looked pretty good, don't you think?" Rachel asked.

"You don't have to keep rubbing it in. I made a big mistake."

"Huge," Rachel told her, nodding in agreement.

"I'm going to fix it right now."

"How?"

"Like I do everything. Make it up as I go along. Wish me luck."

"I'll do more than that," Rachel said, and gave her a hug.

Hailey just hoped she'd be getting a congratulatory hug after the wedding, and not one out of consolation because Nate had turned her down flat.

Nate was waiting against the wall like she knew he would be. He'd always be there for her. She knew that now. Rachel was right. The difference between him and all those other men was that she could depend on him, lean on him. And he wanted her for who she was.

He didn't glance her way, as she took her place beside him. Hailey understood. She'd hurt him. She caught a whiff of his cologne—rugged and masculine and all him. She ached to have his arms around her. To breathe in his scent. To breathe in Nate. The piano music began and the guests stood. Hailey was a huge crier for anything even resembling a wedding, but she stood beside Nate dry-eyed.

Amy looked beautiful dressed in an ivory gown and on her grandfather's arm. Though neither the flowers in her hair, nor the dress or the veil made her truly beautiful. It was her smile. Her smile, knowing she was walking toward the man she loved, and would spend the rest of her life with. Hailey ached to have that, too. To have Nate look at her with the same kind of palpable love Jake's gaze held for Amy.

The music ended, and the guests found their seats.

Her heart began to pound. This was it. If she didn't make her move, didn't give him at least some indication of how she felt, she'd lose him forever.

Don't take no for an answer.

"Dearly beloved…"

Hailey slipped her hand in his.

At her side, Nate jerked in surprise.

He glanced her way. This was the moment she'd been waiting for.

"I love you," she mouthed.

She saw his shoulders visibly relax, a slow smile cross his face. He squeezed her hand. It was all she needed. All that trepidation and angst and worry, man he was easy. A lightness filled her heart.

They returned their attention to the bride and groom, who were now sharing their vows.

Then her tears came. So many times Hailey had wished she'd never met one of those prior duds, but then she would have missed this moment, this feeling with Nate. She could appreciate him the way he deserved to be appreciated.

Amy and Jake kissed and the happy couple walked back down the aisle together. The guests followed them into the Tea Room where the reception would be held. Hailey stayed where she was, never letting go of Nate's hand.

"Do you need to help serve?" he asked.

Hailey shook her head. "We hired extra stuff for that." It was a last minute Rachel idea. Hailey wondered if her sister had guessed she'd changed her mind, knowing that if things worked out with Nate, she'd be too excited over her man to work in the kitchen. And that if things didn't work out, the last thing Hailey would want to do is serve wedding cake.

The bridal party and their families returned to the terrace so the photographer could take pictures.

"Come on," Nate said, and led her down the stairs. At the sand, she kicked off her sandals, and walked beside him. He led her almost to the exact location where they'd first met—where she'd first surprised him with a kiss.

"Tell me," he urged.

"I love you," she said, her smile as wide as it could possibly be. "I love you so much, Nate, and I'm sorry if I hurt you. I was scared."

He brought her into his arms, drawing her to his chest. She heard the solid thump of his heart. "I love you, too." And with those words he placed a kiss on the top of her head.

She squeezed her eyes tight. "I wasn't sure that you would ever say those words to me again, but I grabbed a little insurance just in case."

He looked down into her eyes. Warmth and love turning the gray almost to blue. "What kind of insurance?"

She pulled the familiar red and black card out of the pocket of her skirt. "Your Fate Delivery Card."

"Don't take no for an answer. I should have held on to that, and saved myself a lot of agony."

"But this way I came to you, and you'll never have to doubt me."

"I never doubted you ever," he said against her lips. Then his mouth took over. He ran his tongue along her lips until he sensually slipped it into her mouth.

"I take it this means you're engaged to my sister?" Rachel hollered from the terrace.

Hailey and Nate quit kissing and began laughing.

"So Hailey, will you marry me?"

"Doable," she told him.

* * * * *

MILLS & BOON®
HAVE JOINED FORCES
WITH THE LEANDER TRUST
AND LEANDER CLUB TO HELP
TO DEVELOP TOMORROW'S
CHAMPIONS

We have produced a stunning calendar for 2011 featuring a host of Olympic and World Champions (as they've never been seen before!). Leander Club is recognised the world over for its extraordinary rowing achievements and is committed to developing its squad of athletes to help underpin future British success at World and Olympic level.

All my rowing development has come through the support and back-up from Leander. The Club has taken me from a club rower to an Olympic Silver Medallist. Leander has been the driving force behind my progress'

RIC EGINGTON – Captain, Leander Club Olympic Silver, Beijing, 2009 World Champion.

Please send me ☐ calendar(s) @ £8.99 each plus £3.00 P&P (FREE postage and packing on orders of 3 or more calendars despatching to the same address).

I enclose a cheque for £ _____ made payable to Harlequin Mills & Boon Limited.

Name _____

Address _____

_____ Post code _____

Email _____

Send this whole page and cheque to:
Leander Calendar Offer
Harlequin Mills & Boon Limited
Eton House, 18-24 Paradise Road, Richmond TW9 1SR

All proceeds from the sale of the 2011 Leander Fundraising Calendar will go towards the Leander Trust (Registered Charity No: 284631) – and help in supporting aspiring athletes to train to their full potential.

UNBRIDLED & MIDNIGHT RESOLUTIONS
(2-IN-1 ANTHOLOGY)

BY TORI CARRINGTON & KATHLEEN O'REILLY

Unbridled

Former Marine Carter is staying away from the one thing that's always got him into trouble —women! Unfortunately his sexy new lawyer Laney is making that very difficult.

Midnight Resolutions

A sudden, unexpected kiss between two strangers in Times Square on New Year's Eve turns unforgettable and soon Rose and Ian's sexy affair is red-hot despite the frosty weather...

CHRISTMAS MALE
BY CARA SUMMERS

All policewoman Fiona wants for Christmas is a little excitement. But once she finds herself working a case with gorgeous army captain Campbell she's suddenly aching for a different kind of thrill...

BETTER NAUGHTY THAN NICE
BY VICKI LEWIS THOMPSON, JILL SHALVIS & RHONDA NELSON
(3-IN-1 ANTHOLOGY)

Mischievous Damon Claus is determined to mess things up for his brother Santa. Who'd ever guess that sibling rivalry would result in sensual mistletoe madness for three unsuspecting couples?

On sale from 19th November 201
Don't miss out

Available at WHSmith, Tesco, ASDA, Eas
and all good bookshop

www.millsandboon.co.u

1110/

THE *Balfour* LEGACY

*E*IGHT SISTERS, *E*IGHT SCANDALS

VOLUME 5 – OCTOBER 2010
Zoe's Lesson
by Kate Hewitt

VOLUME 6 – NOVEMBER 2010
Annie's Secret
by Carole Mortimer

VOLUME 7 – DECEMBER 2010
Bella's Disgrace
by Sarah Morgan

VOLUME 8 – JANUARY 2011
Olivia's Awakening
by Margaret Way

8 VOLUMES IN ALL TO COLLECT!

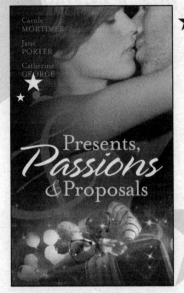
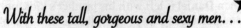

All the magic you'll need this Christmas...

Angels in the Snow

Do fairy lights and family make the perfect Christmas?

Sarah Morgan

When **Daniel** is left with his brother's kids, only one person can help. But it'll take more than mistletoe before **Stella** helps him...

Patrick hadn't advertised for a housekeeper. But when **Hayley** appears, she's the gift he didn't even realise he needed.

Alfie and his little sister know a lot about the magic of Christmas – and they're about to teach the grown-ups a much-needed lesson!

Available 1st October 2010

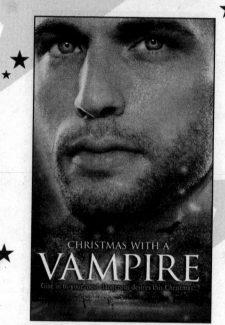

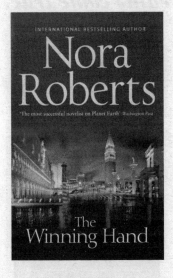

Three heart-warming stories make Christmas dreams come true...

A WINTER LOVE STORY
by Betty Neels

GIVE ME FOREVER
by Caroline Anderson

JED HUNTER'S RELUCTANT BRIDE
by Susanne James

Available 3rd December 2010

2 FREE BOOKS
AND A SURPRISE GIFT

We would like to take this opportunity to thank you for reading thi Mills & Boon® book by offering you the chance to take TWO more specially selected titles from the Blaze® series absolutely FREE! We're also making this offer to introduce you to the benefits of the Mills & Boon® Book Club™—

- **FREE home delivery**
- **FREE gifts and competitions**
- **FREE monthly Newsletter**
- **Exclusive Mills & Boon Book Club offers**
- **Books available before they're in the shops**

Accepting these FREE books and gift places you under no obligation to buy, you may cancel at any time, even after receiving your free books. Simply complete your details below and return the entire page to the address below. You don't even need a stamp!

YES Please send me 2 free Blaze books and a surprise gift. I understand that unless you hear from me, I will receive 3 superb new books every month, including a 2-in-1 book priced at £5.30 and two single books priced at £3.30 each, postage and packing free. I am under no obligation to purchase any books and may cancel my subscription at any time. The free books and gift will be mine to keep in any case.

Ms/Mrs/Miss/Mr_____ Initials _____

Surname _____
Address _____

_____ Postcode _____
E-mail _____

Send this whole page to: Mills & Boon Book Club, Free Book Offer, FREEPOST NAT 10298, Richmond, TW9 1BR